SANTA
Daddy

Allysa Hart
Rayanna Jamison

Prologue
Yule

"Oh good, you're here!" My father's voice was booming and jolly as I appeared in his office, and he welcomed me into his usual bear hug.

"Of course I'm here. You teleported me," I grumbled. "Haven't you ever heard of a text message? Email?"

"This is faster." My father shrugged, taking a seat in his massive red leather chair next to a cozy fireplace.

"Sit, Yule, sit." Yeah, that's right. My parents named me Yule. But, it's really more of a nickname. My real name? Well, that's complicated. It's Santa. Santa Claus. As of today, at least.

Sighing because I knew what was coming, I sat. It wasn't that I wasn't excited about being Santa. It was a pretty damn cool job. It was also a damn overwhelming one, and I knew I was about to undergo orientation. Otherwise known as second-thought central and information overload.

"Now, Yule, as I was saying, I'm glad you're here. As you know, per tradition, tonight, on the eve of your thirty-ninth birthday, I retire, and you take over in my place."

"Yes, sir. I'm aware of the tradition."

My father beamed, stood, and then, with an assured nod, crossed to the antique armoire in the corner of the room. He muttered to himself as he opened drawers and took things off hangers, making a pile in his hands.

Then he turned and held the pile out to me proudly.

"Here you are. Don the uniform, then. It's time to make this official."

I closed my eyes and steeled my shoulders. Making it official was daunting. My father's job was only the most important job in the world. And now it would fall solely on me.

Last minute thoughts aside, I was ready. It was time. I looked at the stack of clothing in my father's outstretched hands and took a deep breath. And then I snapped. One simple snap of my fingers, and that was all it took. The articles of clothing left his hand and took their place upon my body. It was official. I was Santa Claus.

"Oh, no! I missed it? Noel, you were supposed to wait for me," my mother scolded my father as she bustled in with tears in her eyes and a plate full of cookies.

"Well, don't worry, honey. We've only done the official donning of the uniform. There is still the reading of the official Santa code, the factory tour, the elf orientation, and, you know, the talk. I would never do the talk without you."

I raised my eyebrows and regarded them hesitantly. *The talk?* That sounded suspicious. Even more suspicious was the fact that I had never before heard of "the talk" as part of the official passing of the jolliness.

The way my mother blushed and giggled when my father said it, I was reminded of the birds and the bees talk they had given me at the tender age of thirteen.

"Um, guys? Might I remind you that I am thirty-nine years old, a grown man, and I've already been on the receiving end of the talk? It is not an experience I wish to repeat, especially not now."

My father rolled his eyes at me.

"Not that talk. The talk about Mrs. Claus and the *nonbelievers*," he whispered, looking around like someone was going to jump out at him for saying some sort of forbidden phrase.

"I'm sorry? Isn't that two talks? And why are you whispering?"

"Sorry." My father grimaced, looking pained. "Nonbelievers are a tough subject for Santa."

"But, you're not Santa anymore. I am."

"Oh. Right. Well, this should be easier, then."

"Let's get on with it, dear. There's lots to cover before the night is over," my mother reminded him, patting his knee. "And the boy doesn't have much time. Christmas is only two weeks away."

"Right." He nodded at her and turned his attention back to me.

"As you know, Son, there is more to being Santa than making and delivering toys. There is also the mission to rid the world of nonbelievers."

"Yes, I know. It is the job of Santa to bring the magic of Christmas to everyone, young and old, and help to rid the world of nonbelievers because nonbelievers dampen the joy of Christmas for others." I recited part of the Santa code from memory.

"Yes, and..."

"And once I begin working my way through the list of nonbelievers, somewhere in my mission, I will find my Mrs. Claus. Just like you found Mom."

"That's right. Your mother was my thirty-fifth nonbeliever. I found her before my first Christmas as Santa. As you will."

I narrowed my eyes and squinted at him, frowning. "This Christmas? Like the one that is in two weeks? Holy freaking fruitcake! I hope you are kidding me right now! That's impossible. There's no way it will be that easy. And, what if my

Mrs. Claus is not a nonbeliever, and I don't find her in time because all I'm focused on is the mission?"

"She will be, and you will find her. You see, Son, your mother…well, she was not an exception to the rule, she *was* the rule, and failure, my dear boy, is not an option."

"I beg your pardon?"

"Your Mrs. Claus will have been a nonbeliever. She must be. It's in the bylaws. And if you do not make her your wife by Christmas Eve…" He paused and took a deep breath. "Well, let me reiterate, failure is not an option."

"Fabulous," I deadpanned, wondering how many more bombs they planned to drop on me tonight. "Okay, then. This should make for an interesting dating pool. How many existing nonbelievers are women between the ages of twenty and forty? Like fifty? A hundred? Two hundred? A thousand? What are we looking at here?"

My parents exchanged looks before my father turned to me and held up one finger. "One."

"I'm sorry? Did you say one? There is only one nonbeliever left in the whole world?"

"Erm, females in that age bracket, yes. My father pulled an iPhone from his pants pocket and began clicking away at the keys. "This woman." He turned the phone to face me. The woman on the screen was a stunning brunette with skin slightly olive in tone and large chocolate-brown eyes that seemed to sparkle with little flecks of gold in them. At least she was pretty. She was beautiful, actually, and I was getting hard looking at her. "Her name," my father continued, "is Crystal Turner. She's thirty-one years old, and she resides in Las Vegas of all places."

"Oh." I stopped short in my tirade, stunned with this new bit of information. "Well, Kringle Krisps! Okay, then. At least I'm not running around blind. Any tips for how I turn her not only into a believer, but also into Mrs. Claus in two weeks' time? It's not going to be as easy as it was for you with Mom, you know. I can't just turn an unknown woman over my knee and spank her into believing."

My father laughed, a loud guffawing knee-slapping laugh and then, all of a sudden, he stopped and turned very serious. "Well, you could certainly try."

I narrowed my eyes and waited for him to say more, but he remained silent. That was all he had on the subject. Fabulous.

1
Crystal
December 11th, 2018

"Hey! What the hell? How did you get in here? Oh my God! Let me up! Get out!"

One minute I was sitting on my couch, eating popcorn and sipping red wine, watching a documentary on the polar ice caps, and the next minute I was upside down on a stranger's lap, watching my half-Maltese, half-Pomeranian puppy make short work of the spilled popcorn while a puddle of red wine soaked into my brand-new white cashmere rug.

From my precarious position, I craned my neck to peek over my shoulder at my captor. The one who had literally appeared out of nowhere. It was like he had just poofed into my house, and then poof, I was over his knee.

Oh hell no. I was hoping he would at least be hot, or, like, someone I recognized—one of my friends playing some sort of elaborate prank. The guys at the office would totally do something like this. But it wasn't one of the guys from the office. At least, I didn't think it was. It was kind of hard to tell behind the huge white beard and fuzzy red velvet hat. Groaning, I looked down at the fabric of his pants. Yep, red velvet, too.

"What are you doing? Let go of me right now, you jack-hole, and reveal yourself before I call the cops. Marcus, I swear to God, if this is your idea of a joke... I'm not gonna bring you any more pumpkin-spice lattes!"

The bearded intruder did not unhand me. As I watched,

he raised his hand high in the air and brought it down hard against my pajama-clad bottom. That's right, a fucking lunatic dressed as Santa Claus broke into my house and started spanking me.

"Stop! Ouch! That hurts! What do you think you are doing, you fucking lunatic? You are so going to jail!"

"I'm spanking you," the bearded intruder informed me nonchalantly, as if it was no big thing. "You are on my naughty list this year, and worse than that, you're a nonbeliever. Both of those things qualify you for a good spanking. And besides, everyone knows a peppermint mocha beats a pumpkin-spice latte any day."

"Like hell, you delusional prick! The only naughty list you need to worry about is the one in the local paper where they list the names of those who have been arrested, 'cause you're about to be on it. Ooof!"

The dickwad wouldn't stop spanking me. His hand fell across my ass repeatedly while I squirmed, screamed, and squawked. My phone sat on the floor in front of me, at the edge of the slowly spreading puddle of red wine, out of arm's reach.

"Dixie!" I cried, waving at my usually yappy furball of a dog, who was sitting there staring at the scene unfolding like a traitorous vixen. She ignored my cries, like I wasn't being assaulted by some yahoo in a Santa suit going off about naughty lists and peppermint mochas.

"Traitor," I muttered. "See if you get a doggie bag the next time I go to the steak house."

Realizing I was on my own, I tried with renewed vigor to get away, but it was no use. This bearded stranger had a steel grip. It was like there was an invisible vise holding me in place. Yelling and insulting hadn't worked, imploring the help of my worthless guard dog hadn't helped, and getting free of his clutches was a no go. It was time to switch tactics.

"You know," I spoke up, enunciating as clearly as I could through the barrage of steady smacks he was laying across my backside. "If you could please stop hitting me for a second, we could talk this out like reasonable adult people. You are obviously quite upset about something, and while I'm not quite sure what it is or how it has to do with me, I'm willing to listen, and help if I can."

I sounded insanely normal and nice for my situation, but I was desperate and willing to do just about anything if he would stop spanking me. He had been going at it for a good five minutes by now, and it was really starting to hurt!

"Okay, let's talk." He picked me up, lifting me under the armpits, and set me upright on one knee. "Why don't you believe in Santa?"

Dumbfounded, I stared at him, fully aware of the irony in the question. I was sitting on Santa's lap. Nearly thirty-two years old, and this was my first time. "Santa isn't real. Santa is a fairy tale created by major retailers to sell more product and guilt parents into overspending and going into debt each year."

He shook his head, frowning in confusion. "Man, Crystal, someone really did a number on you, didn't they?"

It was my turn to be confused. "Wait, how do you know my name? Damn you, Marcus! I knew it was you, you little prick." Outraged and relieved, I grabbed the bottom of his curly white beard and tugged hard.

"Ouch! Hey! What are you doing? Who's Marcus? You mean Marcus Wheatley? He's on my naughty list, too. But I don't spank the boys. I send Vixen the elf mistress to do that."

Vixen the elf mistress? This was getting far too weird. I tugged his beard again, standing as I did so. The beard was not going to budge.

The mysterious Santa stood, too, pulling his beard from my grasp. "Hey, stop it! It's attached!"

"I see that! What did you do, Marcus? Super-glue it on? I hope you end up with a serious face rash, and Martin from accounting cancels your date. It would serve you right. He's way out of your league anyway!"

"You are crazy," Santa-man muttered. "And quite mean. No wonder you are on the naughty list, if this is how you treat your friends."

I gaped at him. "This is how I treat friends who break into my apartment, start spanking me like a child, and don't come clean once I've caught them red-handed. Now, that's enough, Marcus. I'm done playing. Take off the beard and ditch the costume, or I really am going to call the cops." To drive my point home, I bent down and scooped my phone off the floor.

"Take off the beard, and ditch the costume, hmm? Well, this has taken an interesting turn all of a sudden. Maybe my dad was onto something after all. Very well, then, if that's what you want."

Santa snapped his fingers, and my wish was granted. The beard was gone. Well, not gone. In its place was a sexy salt-and-pepper scruff, and black hair. This man was not Marcus. Not even close.

"Um...you're not Marcus," I stammered, stating the obvious.

"No stinking stockings, Scrooge. Now, what else did you ask me to do? Ditch the suit?" His eyes twinkled mischievously, and I grimaced, my stomach dropping to my toes as I realized what was coming.

"No! Don't!" I yelled, but it was too late. He snapped his fingers again, and poof, no more suit. One second, he was standing there in a full red velvet Santa costume, and the next, all he had on was a pair of candy-cane-striped boxer briefs and a great pair of abs. Holy Hannah.

He was fucking gorgeous. And ripped. And if the bulge in those ridiculous boxers was anything to go by, he was packing, too. Briefly, I considered licking those hard abs, kissing those red lips, and dragging him back to my bedroom. Then I remembered that he was a batshit-crazy criminal who had probably escaped from a mental hospital.

It was a damn shame, too. These days, all the hot ones were taken, gay, or batshit-fucking crazy. Sighing as I gave one last longing look at his washboard abs, I dialed nine-one-one.

"Yes, hello?" I spoke into the phone eying my delusional Santa Claus wannabe up and down, daring him to sneak out now. "I'd like to report an intruder. And, an assault. No, he's still here. My address? Sure, it's seven-twenty-four North Cherry Street."

Santa, or rather the creeper claiming to be Santa, did not look the least bit frightened at the prospect of cops. Ok, so he probably didn't have a record. That was good news for me, but he was in for a rude awakening. Creepy Santa was about to learn that you couldn't break into random women's houses and assault their backsides. It seemed obvious, but there was a serious decline in good parenting these days.

I hung up the phone and narrowed my eyes, peering at his salt-and-pepper beard. Hmm. Dude had to be pushing forty, which meant the decline in parenting probably wasn't the issue. Oh God. My chest seized with fear as I considered a new conclusion. What if he actually was mentally ill? Some sort of asylum escapee? This was a big city. I was sure there were more than a few mental wards in the area. Oh God, why didn't I watch the news?

Santa met my gaze head-on, and smirked. "I'm not a mental patient nor do I come from a subpar upbringing. My parents are quite lovely. And they are looking forward to meeting you. Of course, there is the little matter of the naughty list and the nonbelieving to clear up first, but I'm working on that."

I gaped at him wordlessly, my jaw opening and closing like a fish as I searched my brain for words that were not coming. I was certain that I had not said any of that out loud. And that bit about his parents? Wanting to meet me? What was that about?

Luckily, I was saved from having to voice any coherent thoughts by a knock on my door.

Sticking my tongue out at him, I flung the door open.

"Oh, thank God you're here!" I exclaimed. "Arrest this man!"

Santa

(formerly known as Yule)

Poor Crystal. She was absolutely flummoxed by my mind-reading skills, and she was about to be even more confused when I charmed the kind police officers into going away and leaving me to my business.

Oh well. Confusion looked as good on her as everything else did.

"What seems to be the problem, miss?"

The two men stepped in, and I could tell by looking at them that they were fresh out of the academy. Their baby faces were full of eager innocence, and I was about to blow their minds. What kind of police force paired rookies with rookies anyway?

"This man," Crystal all but yelled with a sweeping gesture in my direction, "appeared in my house out of nowhere and started spanking me!" Her voice was a hushed whisper when she spoke the word spanking, and I had to will my cock not to harden at the sound of her voice saying that sweet word. Spanking her had been much more fun than I had imagined it would be. My father was definitely onto something, not that it was something I wanted to think about, because ew, that involved my mom.

"He appeared? What do you mean, he appeared, miss?" Rookie numero uno had wide bushy eyebrows that formed a caterpillar across the top of his face when he bunched them together in confusion.

"I mean, he just appeared," Crystal repeated, nodding vehemently. "One minute I was enjoying a hearty dinner of popcorn and wine and watching documentaries with my dog, Dixie, and the next, my dinner was on the floor and I'm upended over some lunatic's lap."

"A lunatic wearing candy-cane boxer shorts?" Rookie number two's voice cracked as he tried not to laugh.

"No! No. He was wearing a Santa suit. The full nine yards, with boots, and a fluffy white beard and everything."

I watched two sets of eyes scan the area for said suit. They wouldn't find it. The beauty of Santa's magic.

Their looks of confusion grew. "And that's when he started spa-uhm-assaulting you?" the first cop asked.

"Yes. Exactly. He was assaulting me and going off about naughty lists and nonbelievers and peppermint mochas. He's clearly delusional if not a hardened criminal. Now, go ahead and arrest him! Do your thing. Take him to jail and leave me to my dinner and television."

She actually made a shooing motion with her hands as she said this, and the dark-haired cop raised his bushy eyebrows, looking simultaneously amused and irritated.

"I cannot arrest him for assault, ma'am, without, ahem, evidence of said assault. Did he hurt you? Are there bruises? If so, we will need to step into the other room and document them for our report."

Crystal gaped at him as the meaning of his words sank into her brain. "You mean you want to take pictures of my ass? You cannot be serious!"

She was blushing and sputtering, and I felt bad for her, but the feeling passed quickly. She was, after all, trying to have me arrested.

Rookie cop number two, a freckle-faced ginger who looked like he got straight A's in school and spent his weekends playing Dungeons and Dragons was also red-faced and sputtering as he answered.

"I'm afraid so, ma'am. As my partner said, we can't arrest someone for assault without seeing evidence of said assault."

Her eyes narrowed in anger. "Then arrest him for trespassing! Or breaking and entering!"

"If that's what you want, ma'am, then—"

"It is! It is what I want!" she yelled, not giving him a chance to finish.

"Then you'll have to prove that as well," he finished with a grimace. "Or at least give me more evidence than I am currently seeing."

"Aargh!" Her foot stomped on the soiled carpet as she glared at him. "What kind of cops are you anyway? Fucking bunch of useless morons is what they sent me!"

"The naughty list thing is starting to make sense," I mused aloud, unable to stop myself.

She turned on me then, spinning on her heel. Her eyes lit with rage as she lunged at me, aiming her tiny fists at my chest.

I caught them a split second before she made impact.

"Now, now," I cajoled softly. "Keep that up and you'll be the one going to the pokey for assault, I'm afraid."

Her eyes widened, and her mouth dropped open to form a cute little O of surprise. She looked from me to the cops behind her, an innocent smile on her face.

Both cops stood there with raised eyebrows and their hands on their belts.

The ginger one cleared his throat, and turned our attention back to the matter at hand. "If he broke into your home, ma'am, you need to show us point of entry. A broken window, a busted door, something that corroborates your story."

"But...but... I don't know how he got in! He just appeared. One minute I was sitting on the couch, and the next I was facedown across his lap! I've never seen him before in my life!"

"You said, earlier, miss, that he was wearing a Santa suit, and yet there does not appear to be one discarded."

"He snapped his fingers and then he was down to his boxers," she barked, looking annoyed.

"Okay, miss, exactly how much wine have you had to drink?" the second cop asked, flipping a page in his notebook and scribbling furiously.

Her face went from pale to bright red, and her hands formed little fists at her side. I could tell if I didn't act fast, one of us absolutely would be going to jail tonight, and it wouldn't be me.

"Gentlemen, if we could step outside for a moment," I began, taking my opportunity where I saw it. "I'm sure I can offer an explanation that will get this cleared up in no time."

The two officers nodded, smirking, and I knew exactly what they were thinking. These boys needed to learn a few lessons, or they were destined to become card-carrying members of the good ol' boys club. But that wasn't my problem. Not tonight.

I caught a glimpse of Crystal's face as we stepped outside and shut the door behind us, and I was filled with guilt. What I was about to do was despicable and a blatant abuse of my Santa magic. But the clock was ticking, and I was a desperate man.

2
Santa

With the officers gone, I reentered the house and closed the door behind me, leaning against it. She hadn't locked it, I noted with a smile. Not that it would have stopped me if she had.

"Maybe we should try again," I began, offering my hand to the bewildered Crystal. "I'm Santa, but if you wish, you may call me Yule. I'd ask your name, but I already know it's Crystal Angelina Turner and that you are thirty-one years old. Your birthday is March eleventh, and you were born in Orange County, California. Your parents' names are Maria and Nicholas Turner. Your mother is Hispanic, and your father was Italian." I offered up the little information my father had given me.

Her eyes narrowed, and she refused my offered hand, stepping closer to peer at me with narrowed eyes. "Who are you? How do you know all that? And how did you get those asshole cops to leave?"

"Simple." I shrugged. "I told them the truth."

"What truth?"

"That I'm Santa, and you are my Mrs. Claus."

I could tell she was about to lose it again as she turned away from me and refilled her discarded glass of wine. I watched her pink lips close around the rim as she downed the contents in one large gulp. And I managed to duck before the glass hit the door and shattered mere centimeters from where my head had been.

"That's some arm," I chuckled. "I like your spunk. I'm going to be a very lucky man to have you as my Mrs. Claus."

"Will you stop saying that?" she shrieked. Her gaze darted around the room, and I could see she was looking for something else to throw.

"Okay, okay, okay." I put my hands out in front of me in a gesture of surrender. "Let's start over again, okay?"

I eased away from the door and gestured to the small table in the nook of the kitchen. "How about we sit down and talk? I'm sorry for scaring you and for the way I went about it, but I really do need to talk to you."

She didn't pick up any new objects to hurl at my head, nor did she make a move to lunge at me, so I took her nonanswer as acceptance and slowly made my way to the table, sitting down and waiting for her to take the seat across from me. When she did so, I smiled.

"I don't suppose you have any hot cocoa? Cookies and milk?" I asked, grinning hopefully. I could have made some appear, but I was saving my magical influence for the more important stuff. Plus, I wanted her to offer hospitality. If I could get her to do so, it would make her more amenable to my presence.

At the moment her mouth was set in a thin line, and her expression seemed to say, "Are you for real?"

"I have wine." That was all she said.

"Beer?" I asked hopefully.

She rolled her eyes and heaved a disgruntled sigh but got up from her chair and stomped toward the fridge, returning in a minute with a bottle of imported ale, a bottle opener, and a fresh glass of wine. Wordlessly, she shoved the beer and the opener across the table at me.

"Thank you," I said, popping it open and taking a hearty swig. It was cool and refreshing and did a lot to calm my nerves as I silently cursed my father for his harebrained ideas.

Spanking her had been fun, but spanking her into submission? What had I been thinking, listening to that archaic advice in this day and age?

She sipped her wine then set the glass on the table, twirling it between her fingers as she stared at me.

"I'm sorry I scared you," I said again. "I'm sorry I just appeared in your living room with the halfcocked idea that I could spank you into believing in me. That was stupid and certainly not any way to start a relationship. Although, to be fair, it did work for my parents."

"We are not starting a relationship," she deadpanned.

"We have to," I countered quickly. "It's destiny. I have until Christmas Eve to make you my Mrs. Claus. If I fail…" I furrowed my brow in confusion as I realized I didn't really know what would happen if I couldn't make this feisty woman mine. "If I fail, something very bad will happen to Christmas. It could ruin the holiday forever. Surely you don't want that on your conscience."

"Ruin the holiday forever?" she scoffed. "Is that all you've got? That's pretty vague, and not at all convincing. And newsflash, dude. I don't really care. Christmas is a commercialized holiday made up by toy companies to exploit parents' love for their children. It's complete and utter bullshit."

I had to keep my mouth from falling open in shock as she continued her holiday-hating diatribe. Holy holidays. She wasn't just a nonbeliever. She was a straight-up Christmas hater. This was going to be a lot harder than I'd thought.

"You're telling me that you don't celebrate Christmas, like, at all?" I sputtered, nearly choking on my beer.

"Not at all," she confirmed. "And that's not going to change because some Christmas-loving yahoo shows up in my house in a Santa suit and candy-cane-striped boxers and tells me I should." She sighed. "Listen, dude, besides the assault thing, you're actually pretty nice. I don't know what your deal is, but I can't help you, and even if I could, I don't want to. Please leave."

I rubbed my eyes and tried to dull the pounding in my head. This wasn't how this was supposed to go, and I definitely had worn out my welcome. But I couldn't leave. I had accomplished nothing, made not even the slightest amount of progress.

"I'll go soon," I promised. "I only want to talk. Let's finish our drinks." As I said this, I winked, ever so slightly, and magically refilled my beer to a line just below the brim to buy myself some more time.

"Tell me why you don't celebrate Christmas. Have you ever? When did you stop? What's your favorite Christmas memory?"

"What is this—twenty questions?"

I smiled, and took a sip of my beer. A very small sip.

"I've never celebrated Christmas. I was raised by a single mom who worked hard to make ends meet. My father was killed when I was a baby. On Christmas, of course, and because of that, we didn't celebrate or acknowledge the holiday in any way. At least not as long as I can remember. I was only one the year he died."

I nodded sagely as my gut twisted for her pain. "Did you ever want to? You were just a child, and your friends must have celebrated."

She nodded. "A few times, I wanted to, I'm sure. What kid doesn't want a day of presents for absolutely no reason? But I had a good childhood, and though we struggled, my mom made sure I had everything I needed, and a lot of what I wanted. But it came from her, not some fictional fat guy in an outdated suit."

Her description left a sour taste in my mouth, and I took another sip of beer before answering. "Okay, I get the no

Santa, but Christmas is so much more than presents and a jolly guy in a red suit. What about the rest of it?"

"Like what?"

"A Christmas tree? Cookies? Christmas carols? The season of giving? Candy canes! Reindeer! Elves!"

"I've gone this long without those things. I'm pretty sure I can survive without them now. It's just more commercialism. Why let the toy companies have all the profit? All those other guys wanted in on it, too, and Christmas got bigger and bigger and more over-the-top as the years went by and everyone fought for their piece of the pie."

I shifted uncomfortably in my seat as I mentally acknowledged the truth in her explanation. She wasn't entirely wrong. Christmas had been growing more and more grandiose with each passing year, and the commercialism had gotten a little over-the-top in the last decade or so especially.

"But, the magic," I argued lamely. "There's no replacement for it. You have to experience the magic of Christmas."

"I assure you, I'm fine," she repeated. "Besides, why do you care so much anyway? What does it matter to you if I believe in Santa or celebrate Christmas or experience the so-called magic of the season? What's it to you?"

"It's everything," I stated simply, and it was. Listening to her jaded views on the holiday had me twisted up inside. I could barely stand the thought of her sitting in her house on Christmas day with nothing but a glass of wine and an adorably yappy dog while the rest of the world sat beneath a Christmas tree, opening presents, sipping eggnog, and munching on brightly decorated Christmas cookies.

I finished my beer and stood. "Crystal, listen. I know you don't understand, and I know you don't care, but this is really important to me. Would you please just consider letting in the possibility of change? Could you just open your heart the tiniest bit to the magic of Christmas and see what happens?"

She said nothing.

Son of a nutcracker.

It was a risky move, but I knew what I had to do. I had to leave her something to remember me by.

I snapped my fingers, and a tree appeared in the corner of the living room, covered in colored lights and adorned with red-and-green glass balls. The topper, of course, was a jolly Santa, made to my likeness, with a red velvet suit and real leather boots.

Her eyes widened then narrowed as she scowled at me.

"Pretty, isn't it?" I snapped my fingers again, and a handful of wrapped presents appeared beneath it. "There's gifts in those you know," I whispered. "Technically, you're not supposed to open them until Christmas, but you're already on the naughty list, so I say go for it."

Still nothing. My heart sank, and I realized two weeks may not be enough time. This woman was practically dead inside when it came to Christmas. I snapped my fingers again, going for the full effect this time. Decorations covered every inch of her house now, and a fire roared to life in a fireplace underneath a mantle adorned with festive decor and red velvet stockings that matched my suit.

Instead of looking charmed or excited, she scowled at me. "Will you please knock it off? It's going to take me forever to undo this mess you've made." She stomped her foot. "Stop it right now."

"Not until you agree to let me come back tomorrow and take you on a date. A Christmas date," I elaborated. "It has to be a date doing something Christmasy."

"Ugh, why would I do that?" she groaned. "I don't even know you."

I snapped my fingers again, and the house filled with the smells of Christmas as a tray of cookies and candies and even fruitcake appeared in the center of the table. Next to it were two huge glasses of fresh eggnog.

Her jaw worked back and forth as she took in the fragrant display of delectable treats. She was angry, I could tell, but also tempted. I couldn't blame her. My mother's cookies were pretty fabulous. Crystal stayed strong. I reached over and picked up a cookie in the shape of a tree, groaning loudly as I bit into it.

Chewing slowly and expectantly, I watched her for any sign of breaking, but she gave none.

She was playing hardball. That was fine. I could play, too.

I held my fingers up as if to snap them. "My next two moves are my head elf and a live reindeer. I'd think about giving in if I were you," I warned.

"Oh my God. What is wrong with you?"

I raised my eyebrows and wiggled my fingers.

"Okay, okay! If I admit it is pretty, will you please leave?"

"It's a good start, but I also need you to agree to see me again. More conventionally this time. A date. One where I knock on your door and pick you up. The whole nine yards."

"And then you'll go away and quit snapping?"

"For tonight," I conceded.

"Ugh. Okay, fine. I'll go out with you. Just go away and take this mess with you."

"What mess? I don't see a mess?" I snapped my fingers, but instead of dismantling the decorations, I poofed back into my suit, kissed her cheek, and left the same way I had come in.

3
Crystal
December 12th, 2018

When I walked into the office the next morning, I was wearing a T-shirt and yoga pants with my hair pulled into a messy bun. Thank God for casual Fridays.

Marcus met me at the door with a coffee. "Extra-large double-shot frap with extra whip," he said, holding it out to me, chuckling when I greedily grabbed for it and took a long sip. "And you look like you can use it," he added as we walked toward the elevator.

"You have no idea," I quipped, searching my mind for any part of the night I could share without looking like a certifiable mental case and coming up blank. "I was up really late," I finished with a shrug. It wasn't a lie. It had taken me hours to dismantle the tree, pack up all the decorations and vacuum up piles of pine needles, sprinkles, and glitter. Christmas was messy.

"Girl, same." Marcus sighed, as we rode the elevator to the sixteenth floor. "I'd tell you about my night, but I wouldn't even know where to begin."

He blushed when he said it, and I opened my mouth to tease him and ask what cute boy he'd hooked up with on Grindr, but something stopped me. Usually, Marcus couldn't wait to tell me all about his crazy escapades and the parade of men in and out of his life. He always followed it up with, "Girl, you need to get out there and get you some! You ain't getting any younger."

I knew instinctively that this was not one of these times,

just like I knew now that Marcus had not been behind my late-night visitor.

Santa's crazed ramblings about naughty lists and pepper-mint mochas and Vixen the elf mistress came unbidden to the forefront of my mind, and I pushed them away as I looked at Marcus who was still blushing when the elevator finally stopped. What had Santa said? That he didn't spank the boys? He sent Vixen the elf mistress to do that? I peered at Marcus, suspiciously as we stepped off the elevator. What if I hadn't been the only one with an unexpected late-night visitor last night? I certainly wasn't the only one acting strangely this morning and unwilling to discuss the events that had kept them up late the night before.

I said nothing, sticking my straw in my mouth and sucking to ward off the disturbing thoughts I was having as we walked down the hall.

When Marcus called out a jovial good morning to everyone we passed, including Cindy, the office bitch, I could no longer keep quiet.

"Either you had really good sex last night, or you have completely lost your mind."

Marcus shook his head, looking straight ahead. He was definitely blushing. "Neither. I'm making an effort to be nicer. You never really know what a person is going through in their life. Sometimes a little smile, or a 'good morning' can make all the difference."

Forget Vixen the elf mistress. Marcus had been abducted by aliens.

We parted with a hug then made our way to our separate cubicles, and I sat down at my computer feeling shell-shocked.

Vixen the elf mistress? Marcus was as gay as the day was long, but he was acting completely different. At least I had gotten hot Santa.

Hot Santa who had broken into my house somehow, spanked me, convinced the cops I was crazy, insisted I was his Mrs. Claus, blackmailed me into agreeing to a date by decorating my house like a department store window, and left as mysteriously as he had come.

He was crazy, apeshit bananas, and now I was going on a date with him, and I found myself dreaming about his rock-hard abs, and the generous package that his tight boxer briefs hadn't been able to hide.

It had been a long time since I had been on a proper date, or gotten laid for that matter. No matter how hard up I was, I didn't give it up before the third date, and I didn't make it that far very often. Guys these days didn't seem to be interested in doing things the right way, at least not the ones who were interested in me.

I should cancel the date, I told myself. Nice normal guys didn't break into your home and start spanking you before you'd even been properly introduced. And this guy, Yule, he wasn't nice or normal. But, he did have a certain charm about him, a mischief I could find endearing when it wasn't aimed at trying to turn my life upside down over a stupid holiday. Plus, he was nice to look at. Okay, he was hot. Not that I would ever admit it out loud.

A proper date sounded nice, though, and I'll admit I was curious to see what a "Christmas date" would entail.

He's crazy, I reminded myself, trying to no avail to talk myself out of going through with it. Not that I really had a choice. He didn't leave me his number, and I doubted "Crazy Santa Claus" was listed in the phone book.

Sighing, I began to leaf through my planner to begin my day, startled by faint chimes. I looked down at my wrist and smiled. The charms on my bracelet clinked together, and my insides warmed as I was reminded of the thoughtful gift.

I hadn't been able to throw out the gifts with the rest of

the Christmas paraphernalia he had left behind. Call it the curiosity that killed the cat, but I had needed to know what treasures were hidden in those brightly wrapped packages.

There had been five of them, each more perfect than the last. A gift basket with my favorite wine, chocolates, and bubble bath. A silver bracelet with charms that seemed generic but actually meant a ton to me. A teddy bear, a wine glass, a heart, and a dog. There was, in another box, a designer porcelain teddy bear dressed in a little Santa costume. I collect designer bears, and, of course, I didn't have a Santa one. There was also a throw pillow that said *Bah Humbug*, which had made me laugh, and even a gift for Dixie. A bone, a squeaky toy, and a set of red-and-green bows for her ears.

How crazy Santa knew what to put in those boxes was just another one of his mysteries, and, ultimately, the thing that ensured I would not stand him up.

I'd received a lot of gifts from men over the years, and I knew well enough that choosing the right gift is a talent in itself, and if you find a guy who has that talent, he's probably a keeper.

Dammit. I was going on a date with Santa Claus. Or a crazy person who thought he was Santa Claus, at least. And I was actually looking forward to it.

Santa

"Twelve o'clock cocoa break!" the voice of Rupert, my head elf, boomed over the intercom.

All work ceased around me as everyone scrambled for the break room. The elves took their cocoa very seriously, and, without it, they didn't work half as fast.

I loved cocoa, too, but I didn't drink it all day long as the elves did. During the break, I retired to my office and began to peruse my lists. I had lists for everything, a whole book of them, and keeping them organized and up-to-date was a full-time job in and of itself.

Opening the book to the current naughty list, I zeroed in on the only name that mattered. Crystal Angelina Turner.

Moving her name off this list and off the list of nonbelievers was my number one priority and a task that seemed impossible, given the fact that I had two weeks to accomplish it.

"So, how's it going? You don't have much time left, you know," my father's voice boomed, mirroring my thoughts, and I looked up to see him standing in front of me.

"Argh! Will you stop doing that?" I yelled throwing my hands up in the air. He was teleporting into my office daily, usually to tell me what I was doing wrong. "I'm Santa now, not you. If I needed your opinion, I'd teleport you here and ask for it. It's not supposed to be the other way around."

My father shrugged, looking sheepish for only a moment. "It's an important job. I'm having a hard time letting go. I love you, Son, but I know you weren't given much time. That's why I spent the last two years trimming down the list in that age range for you. Crystal is the best there is. She will make a fine Mrs. Claus, but she's gonna be a tough nut to crack. Speaking of, how's it going with you two?"

"I don't know why you're asking when I'm sure you already know," I grumbled. "It's not going great. She hates Christmas, she called the cops on me, and I barely got her to agree to a date. Not to mention the fact that I have absolutely zero game plan for tonight and only two weeks to make her mine, or Christmas is... Well you haven't exactly told me what happens, but I'm guessing it's pretty bad."

"It is. That's why failure is not an option," my father said, repeating his ominous statement from two nights prior.

"Well, you made it sound like it was going to be easy!"

"With your mother, it was." My father shrugged. "If you had planned ahead and done your homework, maybe last night wouldn't have been such a disaster. But then, you never were much for homework, were you?"

"Homework? What homework?" I shouted, wishing my father would stop talking in riddles, as the bell chimed signaling the end of the cocoa break.

"I've got to get back to work," I growled. "Thanks for all your help," I added, my voice laden with sarcasm.

My father smiled and clapped me on the shoulder. "Read her file, Son. Before your date tonight. The clock is ticking."

Her file. Of course. We had one on everyone. Naturally, with her being over twenty, her file would be archived into storage up on the eighth floor.

Cringle crap. It looked like I would be spending the afternoon in administrative hell. Like I wasn't behind enough. "Rupert," I buzzed over the intercom. "Bring me the keys for the files for the twenty to forty-year-olds, and cancel our inventory briefing today. Email me the numbers instead. I'm on a mission."

"Yes, sir," Rupert squeaked over the walkie-talkie system that allowed him to respond to me wherever he was. "Right away, Santa."

4
Crystal

I hadn't known what to expect on a Christmas date. It certainly hadn't been a ride on a jet-powered sleigh to New York City to see the tree in Times Square, followed by a cozy candlelight dinner of ham and all the trimmings next to a roaring fireplace in a romantic rooftop restaurant while an amazing instrumental quartet played a plethora of Christmas carols nearby.

A sleigh ride. For fucks sake, really?

"I thought the sleigh was only used on Christmas Eve," I questioned. "And where are the reindeer? Another propagational lie?"

Santa, I mean Yule, had a mischievous glimmer in his eye as he lifted his shoulders into a nonchalant shrug. "The reindeer exist, but technology works a little better these days than it used to. I still use them on Christmas Eve, but other than that, they are pretty much retired. As far as using the sleigh for personal use, to be honest, you're probably right. I still haven't finished reading the book of rules and bylaws. This is my first year as Santa, and as was pointed out to me today, I've never been much for homework. Although, speaking of, I did do a little reading up on you today, and what I discovered was very interesting. Very interesting indeed."

I narrowed my eyes, and stopped my fork midway to my mouth. I set it back on my plate, opting instead for a large gulp of red wine.

"Reading up on me? Where?" I questioned, figuring he

must have paid for one of those Internet background searches and berating myself for not doing the same.

Yule finished chewing and swallowed a bite of yams before answering. "Your file, of course."

"My file?" I repeated, as my heart sank into my stomach. That sounded ominous.

"You lied to me, my little elf. Of course, it's not really surprising. After all, you are on the naughty list."

"Oh, will you just stop already with this naughty-list crap? And how are you really accusing me of lying? You're the liar who won't tell me his name!"

Yule sighed and set down his fork. "I've told you many times, though. You choose not to listen, my little doubting elf. My given name is Yule Christopher Claus. The night before last was my thirty-ninth birthday and, as tradition mandates, I officially took over for my father and became Santa Yule Claus. I have not lied one bit. You, on the other hand, told some whoppers last night, didn't you? Keep that up, and the naughty list will be the least of your worries."

I glared at him, and my hand flew to my hip. This dinner conversation had taken a sharp turn, and I was on the defense. "Oh yeah? What lies did I tell, oh jolly one?"

"Oh jolly one?" Yule choked on a laugh. "Oh yeah, that's clever. I've never heard that one before."

The sarcasm was thick and fueled my anger, but I didn't have a quick comeback. "Whatever. Just get to the point. Tell me how I supposedly lied. Enlighten me, Oh great giver of gifts and ho-er of hos."

This time, his laugh was hearty and genuine. "Oh, my little elf. You're going to pay for that one."

I rolled my eyes, and he cleared his throat. I waited.

"Last night, you told me that you had never believed in Santa, not even as a young child." Yule's expression was haughty and expectant.

"Yeah, so?"

"So, when I went through your file, I found not one, not two, not three, but *four* letters to my father, as he was Santa at the time."

My breath hitched in my throat, and my insides twisted at the mention of the letters. There were vague memories of hand-penned notes to Santa, written under the guise of a class assignment. I could have opted out, but I hadn't wanted to. Those letters had been a child's test. I had written them to see for myself who was right—my mother, or the rest of the world around me. In my child's mind, the fact that I never received the one thing I had asked for proved that my mother had been the correct one.

I shook my head to clear the memory and forced a laugh. "So? They were a class assignment. I had to do them. It didn't mean anything."

Yule frowned. "I suspect you are lying again, my little elf."

"Stop calling me that! I'm not little, I'm not yours, and I'm certainly not an elf!"

"Very well, Crystal." He said my name with an edge of sarcasm and distaste that had me yearning for the endearments I had been quick to reject. "Do you remember what you asked Santa for?"

"No," I lied.

He didn't call me on it this time, but his eyes bored into me with a mixture of disbelief and disappointment, and I knew he knew. He took another bite of ham and chewed slowly, then lifted his napkin from his lap and wiped his face with it before throwing it down on the table and leaning back to reach into the breast pocket of his red corduroy blazer. He hadn't worn the Santa suit tonight, and for that I was thankful.

"Let me refresh your memory," he said as he pulled out

four yellowed pieces of paper in different sizes, each folded in half.

I played with the food on my plate, pushing it around like I didn't care, but the truth was I had lost my appetite. My mouth was dry, my palms were damp, and it took a concentrated effort to keep my legs from shaking under the table.

Please don't read them out loud. It was bad enough that he had read them at all, but to hear the childlike pleas spoken aloud would kill me.

I held my breath as he lifted the top sheet and unfolded it, holding it at arm's length in front of his face.

"*December third, 1993*

Dear Santa,

Please bring me a daddy for Christmas.

Love,

Crystal Turner"

My face burned, but I said nothing.

Yule was playing hardball as he lifted the second note from the pile and read it.

"*December fifth, 1994*

Dear Santa,

I have been a very good girl this year. My teacher says I am definitely on the nice list.

I only want one thing for Christmas. A daddy of my very own, to be a husband for my mother. We had a daddy and a husband once, but he died, and I don't remember him much.

It is the only thing I really want.

Thank you.

Love,

Crystal Turner"

I sucked in my lower lip, and tried to hold the tears at bay. "Okay, I get it. I was a dumb kid. Please don't read any more."

"Not dumb. Very sweet. But with an impossible request. Santa Claus is a toymaker, not a matchmaker," Yule joked, trying to ease the tension in the room.

"Touché," I managed. "Okay, well, you read the first two. There's no need to keep reading. The last two are the same as the first."

Yule frowned and picked up the third letter, scanning it as if to see if my claims were true. "They really aren't, though," he concluded. "Each year your request gets longer and more detailed. Sure, the gist is the same, but the letter certainly isn't."

I shrugged, and a tear coursed down my cheek as he read.

"November twenty-ninth, 1995

Dear Santa,

I'm writing earlier this year in case you need extra time to find me a daddy. I don't know how much difference a week will make, but it's the best I can do.

Mom and I are lonely. Especially around Christmas. We don't celebrate, but if we had a daddy, I bet we would.

My friend Emily said since toys are your specialty and not daddies, I should be clearer about what I want.

I don't care what he looks like, as long as he gives good hugs and kisses me on the cheek when he tucks me into bed at night, and a bedtime story would be nice, too, even though my mom usually has that covered.

He should be a little good-looking, though, to keep my mom happy. I've seen pictures of my dad, and he was a very handsome man. My mom has good taste. I'm enclosing a photo so you can see what she likes.

I want him to be nice and loving. He will like to take me out for ice cream and cuddle me on his lap while we watch cartoons together.

But, so I'm not being too unrealistic, he can be stern sometimes if he needs to be, and punish me if I've been naughty. I'll try to be extra good so he doesn't have a reason to. Emily's daddy says daddies don't like to punish their little girls but sometimes they must.

I've been so extra good this year, Santa. This is the only thing I want. I know it's a lot to ask, but it would make me so very happy to have a daddy for this Christmas and always.

Yours truly,

Crystal Angelina Turner"

The tears were falling freely now. I couldn't have stopped them if I tried. I wept bitterly for the lost little girl who had wanted the one thing she had never received. Yule said nothing about my tears, wordlessly handing me a handkerchief from his pocket before picking up the fourth letter.

"Thanksgiving, 1996," he read as I held my breath. This one would be short.

"Dear Santa,

This will be my last letter. If you do not bring me a daddy this year, I will know my mom is right, and you are just a myth.

I want to believe like everyone else does, Santa. Please help me.

Signed,

Crystal Angelina"

He paused, starting to look a little weepy himself. "I can't read the last name because my father's tears smeared the ink."

I wanted to roll my eyes, but I couldn't. "How do you know he cried?" I asked.

"I know him," Yule stated simply. "That, and there is a little note on the bottom in his handwriting."

The image of a big burly Santa crying over a little girl's last letter nearly did me in.

"W-what does it say?" I stuttered.

"It says, *'all I can do is pray.'*"

I nodded, unable to speak, and fidgeted with one of the

charms on my bracelet, without looking to see which one it was.

"I counted several lies, little elf."

I shrugged, not arguing the nickname this time.

"But I'm glad I read your file," he continued, refolding the letters and sticking them back into the pocket of his blazer.

"Why? Because now you know how broken I really am?" I scoffed. "I've got news for you, Santa. I'm not that little girl anymore."

Yule's gaze was sad as his eyes met mine before dropping to my breasts with a mischievous smirk. "No, you certainly are not," he answered with a lascivious grin. "Let me ask you something, Crystal. Did your mother ever remarry?"

"No. She did not."

"So you never got the daddy you so desperately longed for."

"So? Stupid little girl dreams. My mom was more than enough."

"One thing I have learned being Santa and watching my father over the years is that the things we yearned for as children never go away. We may move on, we may outgrow them, we may come to peace with broken dreams, but they never go away."

Date night had certainly taken an interesting turn, and if the conversation didn't take a lighter route here soon, I was going to be a blubbering mess. The problem was, I was incapable of speaking at the moment, and it didn't look like Yule planned to let up. On the contrary, it looked like he was just getting started.

"One of Santa's most classic tricks for turning nonbelievers into believers is to grant and sometimes even re-grant those long-forgotten wishes. Sometimes, like in this case, that requires a little outside-of-the-box thinking."

"Forget it," I sniffled. "There is no 'in this case.' The timeline has long expired. I don't want or need a daddy."

Yule was silent, stroking his beard thoughtfully.

"Not in the traditional sense, no. I'm unable to go back in time and fulfill those little girl desires. But something tells me, little elf, that a daddy and a magical Christmas to go with it is just what you need."

My stomach twisted, and my heart filled with hope. I wasn't about to admit it, but he was right. The long-forgotten desire had never fully gone away. But what did it matter? I was a grown woman. Even if my mom magically found someone and remarried, that man would never fill a daddy role in my life.

"Let me ask you something. Two somethings, actually." Yule's voice was pensive and his expression serious.

"I know you don't know me well, but I think you know that you can trust me, don't you, little elf?"

Dammit. I did. Against all my better judgment and all my adult sensibilities, I knew deep down that Yule Claus, whoever he was, was someone I could trust. "If I didn't know that, I wouldn't be here," I confirmed grudgingly.

Usually, when I went on a first date, at least two people knew where I was and who I was with, and I had an escape plan. I had taken no such precautions with him.

"Okay, second question. This is a hard one. How is it possible with the sleigh ride and those letters and all the Christmas magic you have seen with your own two eyes, you still don't believe that Santa exists, and I am him?"

"It's getting harder and harder," I grumbled. At this point sheer stubbornness was keeping me tethered to my nonbelief. I was thirty-one years old, almost thirty-two, and far too old to start believing in Santa.

Yule was watching me shrewdly, and I got the distinct

feeling that he could see into my soul and hear the things I was not saying.

I met his gaze, and we engaged in a good-old-fashioned staring contest for what felt like a full minute.

Finally, he nodded, stood, and threw some bills on the table. "It's settled, then."

"Wait, what's settled?"

"Give me the weekend, little elf. That's all I ask."

He grabbed my hand and pulled me toward the exit.

"The weekend for what?"

"To be your daddy. To fulfill every abandoned-little-girl desire and to put all your doubts about me to rest once and for all."

This was crazy. He was insane. Be my daddy? What did that even mean? Make me believe in Santa? Why? Why was this all so important to him?

I opened my mouth to answer, and before I could stop myself, I said one word. "Yes."

Yule snapped his fingers, and everything changed.

5
Crystal
December 15th, 2018

When I say everything changed, I mean *everything changed*. Not only did we teleport back to my house, but, apparently, Santa could manipulate time as well. It was no longer the pitch dark of a cold winter night, but the chilly crisp dew of morning could be seen on the trees outside my windows. What the hell?

One minute I was enjoying a ham dinner by a fireplace, in a killer little black dress, and the next, I was back in my bedroom, dressed in a ridiculous pair of pajamas covered in little teddy bears dressed as elves, complete with little elf-shoe slippers that curled up at the ends, pigtail braids, and a fluffy velvet hat, and it was bright outside. What in the ever-loving hell?

And where was Santa? He had left me emotionally wrung out with those letters, gotten me to agree to participate in yet more of his ridiculous antics, teleported me home and into this ridiculous getup, and then disappeared?

Oh hell no. "I should have said no," I grumbled to Dixie who was currently oblivious to all the craziness around her. *What was I thinking?* I mentally berated myself. *Even if he really was Santa, he couldn't do anything to change the past. I'm in my thirties, not some six-year-old child. I don't need a Daddy.* I was heated now, stomping around the room with such fervor, I nearly tripped over my own feet, thanks to the ridiculous slippers I was wearing. Shrieking, I sat on the edge of my bed and ripped them off my feet,

hurling them across the room with a satisfied grin. That
was slightly better, I thought, as they hit the mirror on my
closet door. I caught a glimpse of myself and rolled my
eyes. I looked ridiculous. Flinging off the hat, I went for
the braids next. Carefully undoing the perfect plaits, I
fluffed my hair and pulled it back into my favorite messy
bun. The next thing to go had to be these ridiculous
pajamas.

Already feeling more like myself, I pulled open the
bottom drawer of my dresser, and rummaged through my
favorite lounge clothes, pulling out a pair of yoga pants and a
shirt from a local bar that had a drawing of two monkeys
doing it. That was more like it. Far more apropos of a thirty-
one-year-old professional woman.

I was thinking maybe a shower before I changed, to wash
off the tears I had cried and the stench of ridiculousness I was
currently feeling. I grabbed a fresh bra and panties from my
top drawer and padded toward my adjoining bathroom. I
shut the door behind me and had put my hand on the
shower faucet when I heard him bellow my name. Well, my
name, and that ridiculous nickname he insisted on calling
me. He announced gleefully that breakfast was ready.

So, he was here. And apparently, he had cooked breakfast. *What the hell?*

I contemplated ignoring him and seeing how long it
would take him to disappear, but curiosity got the better of
me again. Exactly what did he have planned anyway? I had to
know. I had agreed to some Christmas magic Daddy
weekend thing, and I was going to stick it out.

At least for the weekend. Come Monday, I was changing
the locks, putting bars on the window, and figuring out some
way to proof the place against magical mystery men who
seemed to pop in and out at will.

He called for me again, and I sighed, turned off the

faucet, and padded down the hall. I was in too far to quit now.

Santa

Watching her emotional reaction as I had read her forgotten letters out loud had almost been my undoing. Getting through dinner without throwing them down on the table and pulling her into my lap had taken every ounce of strength and self-control I currently possessed, but I had needed that kind of emotionally gutted reaction from her. It told me that my plan, however unconventional, was on the right track. When I decided we would have a Daddy weekend, the idea had touched my soul and left me feeling warm and protective. By the time I had been through planning out details before our date, I was sure that I wanted it more than she needed it. But she did need it. Of that I was certain. That desperate little girl inside her was alive and well, and as soon as I got through the tough outer shell, the rest would be like feeding carrots to a reindeer.

I sipped my coffee as I flipped the last of the pancakes then turned around to survey my handiwork. Something about actually cooking the breakfast, instead of making it magically appear, was satisfying. I hoped my little elf appreciated it once she recovered from the time manipulation and switcheroo I had pulled on her. "Crystal! It's time for breakfast, my little elf!" I hollered down the short hallway, keeping my eyes on the breakfast table.

The table was full of festive decorations and delicious breakfast offerings. I had whipped up a huge stack of fluffy pancakes, a pile of crisp bacon, and half a dozen perfectly prepared eggs. And, of course, hot chocolate with tiny Christmas tree marshmallows. It looked like my mother's table every Christmas afternoon when my father finally woke up after sleeping off his long night of deliveries. The only problem was the rest of my decorations from my first visit had disappeared. I had known they would, of course, but it was still disappointing. My little brat had boxed everything up and put it out with the trash, but a simple snap brought the boxes all back to me. It actually worked better this way because now we could decorate together. It was part of the fun.

"What the fuck?"

I cringed when I heard the vulgar language coming from behind me. "That will have to be the first lesson you learn, my little elf. Christmas and cursing do not go together. We don't use that kind of vulgar language at the North Pole. If you must cuss, say things like son of a nutcracker, or jingle balls, or cringle crap."

"Cringle crap? Jingle balls? You're out of your mother-fucking mind."

The thought of spanking her sexy backside again had my cock twitching with excitement, but the juxtaposition of her filthy mouth and the adorable little Christmas pj's I had picked out melted that fantasy from my mind, and I was back in Daddy mode. She looked adorably cozy covered from neck to toe in teddy-bear elves.

"I may be out of my merry fruitcaking mind, but you, little elf, are getting a spanking. Right after we eat."

Her eyes widened as she took in the breakfast table.

"Oh God. I'd hoped it was a dream, but it's like every time I wake up it gets worse and worse," she mumbled as she made her way to the coffeepot, turning to glare at me when she found it empty. "All this and you couldn't have made coffee? What the hell is wrong with you?" She shook the empty pot in my direction.

"Actually, I did make coffee. I made it and then I drank it. Your hot cocoa is on the table."

"I don't drink hot cocoa. I am not a child. I want coffee. I need coffee to deal with life in general, but with all this," she hollered, flailing her arms at the table, "I'm going to need the coffee strong as shit with some Bailey's Irish Cream topping it off."

"What kind of Daddy would I be if I allowed my little girl to drink coffee or alcohol?" I questioned, shaking my head at her as I inwardly chortled at her coffee-craving rant. This was going to be far more difficult than I had originally anticipated. That just meant it would be far more rewarding as well. "You need to stop cussing at me, little elf, or there will be consequences." I quirked my brow, subtly reminding her of our agreement.

She rubbed her temples. "I cannot with you right now. This is too much. I went thirty years without a father. I do not need one now!" She balled her fists at her sides and stomped her foot before turning around and opening the cupboard above her. "Where is my coffee?" she snapped.

I crossed my arms and steeled myself for her tantrum to reach epic proportions. "It's put away. You will not be having any coffee this weekend, little elf. You agreed to give me the weekend, and that is my decision. No coffee. Not now, and not later."

"Fuck you and the fucking reindeer you rode in on. I'm an adult, and I can have coffee if I want to. Give it back right now!" she shrieked, stomping her feet like an overtired toddler.

I unbuttoned the sleeves of my flannel shirt and rolled them up to my elbows as I listened to her continue her tirade about domineering fake Santas taking over her life. I was about to show her exactly how Santa felt about her behavior, but I gave her one more chance to redeem herself. "Crystal, you have already earned a spanking for your language and your behavior. And now it will be happening sooner rather than later."

She stopped yelling long enough to pick up a coffee mug and hurl it in my direction. I caught it in midair and set it on the table between us before advancing on her. She could see from my expression that I meant business, and she quickly backed away, her eyes wide.

"Don't you dare!" she yelled as she backed away as quickly as I advanced. Before she could run, I grabbed her arm. She turned to punch me, but I ducked and threw her over my shoulder. Carrying her back into the bedroom, I peppered her backside with some warning swats. "This is not how I wanted to start our special weekend, little girl, but your behavior is deplorable, and Daddy does not appreciate it."

"You are not my father!" she yelled, kicking her feet in the air and slamming her fists into my back.

As soon as we were in her room, I sat down on the bed and set her on her feet in front of me. Keeping a tight hold on her hands, I channeled my own father and gave her the sternest look I could muster. "You're right. I'm not your father. I wish I could bring him back for you, but I cannot. However, you agreed to let me be your Daddy for the weekend to introduce you to the magic of Christmas, did you not?"

She tugged her arms, testing my hold. "You tricked me. You didn't tell me about any of this."

"I also didn't tell you I was taking you on my sleigh or any of the other things that occurred last night, and you didn't complain."

"That was different." She pouted.

"Was it? You had no control of where we went, what we did, or what we ate. I took care of everything just as I have this morning." Her resolve was melting. She wanted this badly, I could tell, but she was having a hard time letting go of her control. A spanking would help to get her in the mindset I needed her to be in to get the most out of everything I had planned for us this weekend.

"But you took my coffee." Her arguments were getting weaker by the second, and her shoulders sagged.

"Coffee isn't good for little girls."

"But I'm not a little girl."

"You are my little girl this weekend," I said firmly, determined to stop the coffee argument before it got too out of hand. "I am your Daddy, and I am going to take care of you as such. I'm going to spoil you thoroughly. We are going to do all of the things you ever dreamed about doing with your Daddy and then some." I let go of one of her hands, smiling when she did not try to run again, and pulled the folded letters out of my pocket. Holding them up between us I threw out my Hail Mary. If she was still reluctant to continue, I wasn't sure how I would move forward. "The little girl from these letters still lives in here." I tapped her chest with the papers. "And she deserves to experience the magic of Christmas with a loving Daddy, doesn't she?"

I sent up a silent thank you when Crystal sighed and nodded, tears filling her eyes.

"Will you let me be that Daddy, little elf?"

Crystal

What are you doing, Crystal? Bail now! Tell him he's nuts, and you want nothing to do with any of this! "Yes." *No!*

"Thank you, sweetheart." He put the letters next to him on the bed and pulled me into his lap. Why I wrapped my arms around him and cuddled in tight, I will never know, but I did and it felt…right.

"I have completely lost my mind," I mumbled into his chest, and he chuckled.

"Not so, little elf. Now, let's handle our business, and then we will eat breakfast. You are going to need lots of energy for all of the activities I have planned."

"What business?" I peered up at him suspiciously, but I was pretty sure I knew exactly what he was referring to.

"I told you. You've earned yourself a spanking."

"I hoped that was an empty threat."

"Daddies don't make empty threats, little one. They make promises, and they keep them. And my promise to you is this: You are going to learn about the magic of Christmas either on my knee or over it, little elf."

I groaned and held his neck tighter when I felt him try to lift me off his knee. "I don't want a spanking." I faintly remembered the sting from my unexpected first trip over his knee.

"You should have thought about that before you threw a tantrum." He peeled my hands from behind his neck and stood me in front of him once more. "My little elf does not say naughty words. She does not demand things after Daddy has already said no. She certainly does not throw things at her Daddy. If any of those things happen again, this spanking will feel like a holly-jolly love tap, understand?"

I covered my face in embarrassment. I had done all of those things, but in my defense, I was uncaffeinated. "I wasn't thinking because I didn't have coffee."

"Well, you need to learn to control that temper and that

mouth. Clean up your language, or I will clean it up for you, with a bar of soap."

Covering my mouth, I shook my head vehemently. He had no idea what he was asking. I'd been cussing since I was ten. My mom had the mouth of a sailor, and she never cared much about it. How the heck was I going to quit?

"This will leave you with a nice reminder to watch your mouth," Yule said with a chuckle as he pulled me over his knee. He had done it again, I noted. I was going to have to be very careful around this man as it seemed he could read my mind.

Once he settled me over his knee, reality set in. I was going to be spanked like an errant child. My only experience with spanking was the abrupt assault on my backside that marked the moment we met.

"Wait!" I yelled a split second before his hand came crashing down on my pajama-covered bottom. "Let's talk about this!"

He didn't stop, didn't even pause. His hand fell hard against my rear five more times before I even got the words out.

He did however, address my protest. "There is nothing to talk about, little elf. You agreed not once, but twice to have me as your Daddy for the weekend, did you not?"

"Yes! But…" Spanks continued to rain across the center of my upturned bottom, and I gasped for air as I tried to push words out between the stinging blows.

"As your Daddy, I have certain duties. I plan to love and spoil you with a weekend you will never forget, but I also plan to hold you accountable to the rules I would hold a little girl of my own to. For the remainder of the weekend, in order for this to work, you must consider yourself no older than six, and I must treat you as such."

He paused then, and began to rub my backside, which already felt tender and bruised from his ministrations.

"What? That's preposterous! I'm not six, I'm thirty-one!"

"It's called age play, or regression, depending on who you ask, and it's actually a very effective form of therapy," Santa informed me matter-of-factly.

"Grrrr."

"I can see that it hasn't started to work yet." His hands left my bottom, and I peered over my shoulder to see him tapping his chin thoughtfully. "I think," he mused, "that if I had my own little girl of six, and I was trying to teach her a lesson that wasn't quite sinking in, I would make sure it did, by way of a sound bare-bottom spanking."

I watched in horror as he reached for the waistband of my ridiculous pajama bottoms.

Without waiting for my consent, or my argument, he pulled them down, and my panties with them, exposing my bare bottom. I gasped as the cool air from the overhead fan hit my sore flesh, and the breeze did things to my girly bits I'm not even going to talk about. *How mortifying.*

He lifted his hand once more, and I screamed. It was the wrong thing to do. His expression grew hard, and he began to spank with a renewed vigor. It hurt so much more on the bare.

"As per your letter, little one, let me remind you, 'A daddy can be stern sometimes if he needs to be, and punish me if I've been naughty. I'll try to be extra good so he doesn't have a reason to. Emily's daddy says daddies don't like to punish their little girls but sometimes they must.'"

Every single word he recited back to me was punctuated with a swat, and each swat felt harder than the one before until I couldn't take it any longer. His words combined with the stinging pain of his hard hand across my bare ass broke me. My entire body sagged over his knee, and I cried. I cried harder than I had in years. This man, whoever he was, was doing things to my mind and body that I simply did not appreciate. Yet, I craved it. As angry as I was, and as ridiculous and unbelievable as this all seemed, I wanted everything he was offering. I wanted him to be my Daddy. I wanted him to hold me accountable. I wanted everything he promised me.

I'm not sure when the spanking stopped, but when I finally caught my breath, I noticed he was stroking me tenderly, his cold hands a balm against my heated backside.

"You're a good girl, little one. Daddy is going to take good care of you, I promise."

"O-o-okay," I agreed between sobs. "I-I-I'm sorry for being s-s-so bad. I d-d-don't even want coffee any m-m-more."

I could hear him trying not to laugh as he lifted me onto his knee and hugged me tight. "This was never about coffee, little elf. This is about control. You need to learn to give me the reins for a while."

I giggled at the irony of his statement. "How come you always get to drive the sleigh?"

"Because I'm the Daddy, and you are the pampered little girl. Now, are you ready to have some breakfast?"

"No, my butt hurts."

"Well, I would hope so. You took a good long spanking that you will hopefully feel all day. I don't want to have to do that again. But your butt hurting will not keep you from filling your stomach." He stood me up and righted my pants and panties. "Now, let's go eat, and then we will go get us a tree."

I held back the groan about the tree but just barely. He was going to make it look like Christmas threw up in my house again, except this time he was going to make me help him do it.

6
Santa

"Couldn't you conjure up a tree like you did before? It's freezing and way too naturey out here."

"Real Daddies don't use magic. Real Daddies do things the hard way."

"Yeah? Is that why you flew us here in a sleigh with heated seats and a cocoa dispenser?" Crystal scoffed, her voice a mixture of mirth and annoyance.

"That's different," I argued, but she was right. Vegas had been seriously lacking in their tree selection, so I'd flown us to a farm where we could choose and chop down our own. "It's about the experience, little elf. How's this one?"

"It looks the same as the one next to it. Pick one! I want to get back to the heated seats."

I'll heat your seat, I thought, growing hard at the memory of her bottom growing red under my hand. *Down boy.* This weekend was not about sex. It was about anything and everything but. God willing, the sex would come later.

"You can't just pick one," I grunted, willing my brain to return to the subject at hand. "It has to be the right one."

"I can't feel my toes," she whined, following me down a row of thick elms and majestic firs. "Fine, how about this one?" She pointed to a robust noble fir that stood at about six-and-a-half feet tall. It had a fluffy body and sturdy branches, perfect for decorating.

"Good choice. Do you want to help me cut it down?" I

held the saw out to her, but she jumped back as if it were going to bite her.

"Umm, do Daddies let little girls play with sharp saws? That doesn't seem safe."

When she said Daddy like that, I had hoped it was a sign, that she was beginning to soften and embrace her inner child. Then I caught a glimpse of her face and realized she was simply bratting. But bratting was good. I could work with bratting. Baby steps.

"You don't want to get dirty, is that it?"

"This jacket is brand new and expensive. There's no way I'm getting down in the dirt."

I shook my head and lay on the ground under the tree.

"Yule, for God's sake, just wiggle your nose and uproot the sucker. Enough with the hard way. You're going to chop off a finger or something under there."

Ignoring her protests, I sawed through the narrow trunk enough so that I could climb out and push it over. "There, see? I even have all of my fingers still."

"Fabulous. Can we go now?"

"Yep. Everything else we need is already at your apartment." I hefted the tree onto my shoulder and began my trek back to the sleigh. "Next up on our Christmas fun day, tree decorating!"

"Oh goody," she quipped, looking as if I had announced that our next plan was a trip to the dentist's office.

I heaved a sigh. This was not working the way I wanted it to. I wanted her to enjoy the process, not feel as though she were being tortured.

"Actually, change of plans. I have a surprise for you. We aren't going back to your house quite yet."

"Please tell me it's somewhere warm and clean."

"Yes, my prissy little elf. No more nature for you."

"Yay!" She clapped her hands and ran ahead of me to the sleigh. *Well, that was easy.*

I sent the sleigh and tree home before teleporting us to a mall near her apartment. There were not many places to hide a sleigh in a busy mall parking lot.

"Oh, I love this place!" she exclaimed when she saw where we were. "They have the best stores and an amazing restaurant called Malibu that puts those cute little umbrellas in your cocktails." She smiled, and I saw the flicker of excitement for the first time since this morning. Apparently stores, restaurants, and shopping were the way to my little elf's heart, and nature was a no go. I made a mental note of her preferences as she grabbed my hand and pulled me along.

"Well, hold your reindeer, now. There will be no cocktails today, little elf."

"I know, I know. Party pooper." She scrunched up her nose and stuck the tip of her tongue between her lips, but she was smiling and still seemed excited at the prospect of being here with me. She was comfortable enough to tease, if not to completely let go. I'd take it.

"Poor thing." I pinched her cheek, teasing back. "I have something more fun in mind."

"What's more fun than cocktails?"

"Teddy bears."

She stopped dead in her tracks and turned to look back at me with an expression of awe and suspicion. She was staring at me like I held the secrets to the universe.

"How did you know I collect bears?"

"I'm very observant," I said with a wink. "You collect porcelain designer bears, and they are beautiful, but what we are getting is a cuddly teddy bear. One that you can hug whenever you want." I tugged her hand gently to get her moving again.

"I've never had a teddy bear," she admitted quietly.

"I know. You surround yourself with bears you can't touch, snuggle, or play with. That ends today. Every little girl deserves a teddy bear." Picking up the pace again, I led her through the mall to the teddy-bear store. It was the chain one where she could choose any bear she wanted, stuff it, and even pick out a special outfit for it. A perfect activity for a Christmas-magic weekend. At the entrance to the store, she froze again and bounced on the balls of her feet, excitement washing over her features as her gaze darted all over the store.

"I've always wanted to do this," she admitted, "but it's silly. I'm too old for this stuff." Her words said one thing, but her entire body was vibrating with an excitement she could not hide. She was so close to letting go, and I hoped this would be the activity that sent her over the edge.

"Don't be silly. You are never too old for anything. Come on. You can pick any one you want." I led her to the wall that showcased a plethora of fuzzy critters to choose from, and she went straight to the bears section. I watched with interest and tried to guess which one she would pick. I could hear the thoughts bouncing around in her head. She wanted the glittery tie-dye bear, but she kept going back to the plainer ones, probably telling herself they were more suitable.

"Pick the one you want and stop thinking about anyone else," I encouraged her. I wasn't going to force her, but I hoped she allowed this for herself. It was obvious she wanted it.

"This one has a sweet smile." She picked up the white bear and gave it a once-over. Glancing back and forth between it and the tie-dye one, she set the bear down again. "This is too hard." She shook her head and looked at me.

Frustrated tears filled her eyes. She was at war with herself, and she didn't know how to let go.

"It is definitely a hard choice. How about this, why don't you choose two, and we can put one in the donation bin on our way out? That will give you some extra time to make up your mind."

She smiled at the suggestion and instantly picked up the tie-dye bear and the white one she had held before. "That's a great idea! Kids love colorful stuff, right? They would want this guy."

I tried to hide my frustration and sadness at her answer. She wasn't going to give in and take what she wanted. "I'm sure they will be thankful for either one. Let's get them stuffed and dressed before they get cold," I teased, tickling her from behind to get her moving.

"Mommy! Mommy! That man is Santa Claus." *Uh oh.* I'd been spotted. Some intuitive child would pick me out of a crowd every time I went out. I smiled in his direction as his mom tried desperately to pull him away. "Santa! I've been the goodest boy this year," he announced to everyone within earshot.

"I'm proud of you, buddy. Keep up the good work," I called back. I couldn't help myself. He brightened up and allowed his mom to pull him from the area. I turned to see Crystal watching me in disbelief, hugging both unstuffed bears to her body. "What can I say?" I shrugged, and she shook her head with a smile.

We spent another hour in the store choosing outfits for the bears. Interestingly enough, she dressed the white bear as a cowgirl, but she dressed the tie-dyed one in a Santa suit, claiming it was what the children would want. I went along with it, happy that she was enjoying herself. Time would tell if she could truly let go and choose the one she wanted.

"Are you hungry, little elf?" I asked, as I paid for the bears. The girl behind the counter giggled.

"That's the cutest nickname I've ever heard."

I watched Crystal out of the corner of my eye. She tensed slightly but bounced back fast. "The man has a Santa complex," she said with an exaggerated sigh and an eye roll as she walked out of the store.

I couldn't help but laugh as I followed her. "A Santa complex, huh?"

"Well, what else would you call it?"

"I *am* Santa. There's no complex about it."

"Oh, it's all the complex, trust me. And yes, I'm hungry."

I shook my head but let it go. "All right, you mentioned a good restaurant. Let's go there."

The restaurant she mentioned was an amazing cantina of authentic Mexican, with a lovely little balcony that overlooked the Las Vegas Strip, and the fruity drinks certainly did look tempting. We would have to come back another time, when she wasn't supposed to be six. But she was right. The food was delicious, and it was a good choice for lunch. We both left thoroughly satisfied and headed to the other side of the mall where the toy-donation bin was located. To my delight it was right next to the mall Santa.

"Look, everyone who donates gets a free photo!"

"I don't need a photo with a fake Santa Claus," she dead-panned, staring at me with disbelief.

"Of course you do. It's part of the fun of Christmas. Come on." I took her hand and pulled her to the line.

"This is not happening. I am not sitting on the knee of some crazy man in a red suit."

"Would you rather go over Daddy's knee instead?" I whispered close to her ear. She shivered and shook her head. "Well then, looks like you're going to have to figure out what you want for Christmas and tell Santa. You're next." I took the bear boxes from her hands and nudged her forward. Reluctantly, she stepped toward the jolly old man. He was a fair replica, one of the better ones I'd seen, if I do say so myself. Not that it mattered to Crystal as she stepped forward with an expression of chagrin.

"Sorry, I know I'm too old for this."

"Nonsense, young lady. No one is too old for Christmas," Fake Santa boomed in a jovial voice. He was very convincing as Santa and reminded me a lot of my father. He held his hand out to her, and she let him guide her onto his lap. She sat slowly, but I watched as he charmed her and eventually even made her smile. This guy was good. I needed to take some lessons. She leaned up and whispered in his ear before posing for the photo and accepting the mini candy cane he offered from a sack near his chair.

Mall Santa winked at me. "This one is a handful."

"You have no idea," I answered with a wink as well, turning to Crystal. "What did you ask him for?"

"That's between me and Santa." Her tone was full of sass and spunk, and I was grateful to see she had loosened up again.

The little smile didn't leave her lips until we got to the donation bin. I silently handed her both boxes not wanting to influence her choice. Whatever she did, I hoped it made her happy.

She opened both boxes, peering inside to see which bear lay hidden behind the cardboard. She sighed softly and gently placed one of the boxes in the bin.

"Good girl," I muttered and kissed the top of her head. "Now, let's go decorate our tree."

Turning a corner, so we were out of the public eye, I snapped my fingers and teleported us back to her apartment.

Crystal

Weirdest day ever.

I wasn't sure what Yule had had in mind for this weekend, or if he actually thought I could magically get to a place where I was mentally six, but something was definitely happening to my psyche. My emotions were all over the place. I went from annoyed to excited and back again so many times I could have made Dr. Jekyll and Mr. Hyde proud.

As soon as we left the mall, I was bummed out again. I had so much fun choosing and dressing the bears, and using Mall Santa to tease Yule had been a brilliant plan on my part. It was driving him crazy not knowing what I had asked Santa for.

Yule's idea of donating a bear had been a great one, but I'd let my brain get the best of me and made the wrong choice. Santa bear was sitting all alone in that toy bin, and I wanted him back. My disappointment must have been evident on my face, as Yule came over, and rubbed my back, peering into my eyes.

"What's wrong, little elf?"

"Nothing," I lied. "I'm just tired. It's been a long day." It had been a long day. Especially with Friday night magically morphing into Saturday morning, after I had barely slept on Thursday night.

"How about a nap?" It was framed in a suggestion, but I was sure he didn't mean it as such.

"If I take a nap, I will not be able to sleep tonight. It's a curse," I told him truthfully.

"Okay. Well then let's settle in and move to the next thing on Daddy's agenda, shall we?"

"What's that?"

"Hot cocoa and one of my favorite Christmas movies! We can string popcorn for the tree while we watch."

"Okay," I sighed. I was on Christmas overload, but I could probably zone out while doing the popcorn. Yule hooked his finger under my chin and looked into my eyes. "What's going on, sweetheart?"

"Nothing, it's stupid. Let's do your movie and whatever."

He wasn't having that, and before I could blink, he had me cuddled on his lap on my overstuffed sofa. "Tell me the truth, little elf, and before you tell me it's nothing again, you should think about the fact that lying to Daddy is against the rules and will earn you a hot bottom and a mouthful of soap."

I grimaced at the threat. The pain from my earlier spanking had definitely faded, but I could still feel the effects of it, and I certainly didn't want another one. "Soap isn't in my diet plan," I said with a sarcastic undertone.

"Well, then, choose your words wisely, little girl."

"Seriously, you want to know what's wrong? You have me all confused inside, and now I'm pining over a stupid bear. That's what's wrong. Happy?" I tried to push off his lap, but he wouldn't let go, so I crossed my arms over my chest and turned away from him as best I could.

He sighed behind me. "What am I going to do with you?"

"You could drop all of this, and we could just date like normal people?" I asked hopefully, a little surprised that I left dating on the table. I was starting to really like Yule. He was sexy as hell, and his joy for life really lifted my spirits. Besides this whole Santa gig, he was practically the perfect man.

"What kind of Daddy would I be if I gave up?" Yule's

eyes sparkled mischievously when he looked at me, and his grin was the cat-that-ate-the-canary type. "Why don't you grab the bear box and bring it over here? Let's see if you still feel the same after you can give your bear a cuddle."

I got off his lap and retrieved the cardboard package shaped like a house before returning to the couch, opting to sit next to Yule instead of on him. I did my best to ignore my longing to once again be in his arms.

We both sat silently for a moment. I didn't want to open the box. I didn't want to want the bear that was inside, didn't want to be hit with the disappointment I knew was in store. And I was mad at myself, too, for being so ridiculous. I was a grown woman, and I was sad that I had picked the wrong teddy bear. Yule set his hand on my thigh and gave a squeeze.

"He's probably lonely all stuffed in that box."

I smiled and rolled my eyes but reached up and opened the top. Confusion washed through me as I pulled out the tie-dyed Santa bear. "What? How?" I shoved back the overwhelming emotions, refusing to show how overjoyed I was to see the colorful stuffed animal.

"Your Daddy is Santa Claus, little one. Anything is possible."

"No. This is too much. This is all too much." I shoved the bear back inside its house and forced it closed. Setting it down on the couch between us, I got up and stomped to my bedroom, slamming the door behind me.

Throwing myself facedown on the bed, I covered my head with my pillow and screamed. It was better than the alternative of crying. I wasn't angry, just overwhelmed. My world had been flipped upside down, and there was no way I could flip it back. Yule made me yearn for things I had long since given up on. Growing up without a father had been difficult, but I had learned to cope. My mother was wonderful and loved me with all her heart. She made sure my every need was met, but a little girl needs a father. I needed a father. Now I had this man in my life calling himself Daddy and opening emotional doors that I had locked tight. *Ugh.*

"Little elf," Yule spoke through the door. "Are you okay?"

I didn't answer, mainly because I didn't know the answer. *Yes? No? I feel more alive than I have in years, and it scares me?* What was I supposed to say?

The door creaked open. I couldn't see him, but I heard his footsteps approach the bed and then the side of the mattress sank with the weight of his body. He rubbed my back but said nothing. His touch was comforting and reassuring, and his mere presence settled my soul.

"I don't know how to process all of this," I finally admitted as I lifted the pillow off my head.

"You're thinking too much, little one. You need to relax and let go. You need to trust me."

"It's harder than you make it sound."

"No doubt. So how can I help?"

"That's just it. It's not you. You're doing all the right things. You're like the perfect man, aside from this crazy obsession with Christmas."

"I'm Santa. Christmas is kind of my gig."

I groaned and dropped the pillow back on my head, talking through the fabric and not caring if he could understand my words or not, "I know. I know. I don't even hate it as much as I thought I would, but we can't keep going like this."

"Like what?"

"This Daddy stuff. I can't handle it. It's too much."

He lifted the pillow and tossed it onto the other side of the bed. "Little elf, you promised me the weekend. Are you reneging? Is that really what you want?"

Yes. "No."

"I didn't think so. So, here is what we are going to do. We are going to watch some silly Christmas classics while we string our popcorn, then we are going to flip on some Christmas tunes, enjoy a nice simple dinner, and decorate that amazing tree you picked out. After all that, we will get you ready for bed and call it a night. And we'll do all of that because Daddy wants to spoil his girl and enjoy the time we have together. Okay?"

"Can we not and say we did?"

"Can I redden your tail and then do it all anyway?"

"No, thank you."

"Well, then, it's settled. No more moping, just relax and let go. You will be surprised how much fun you can have."

7
Santa

I took a step back and surveyed our handiwork. The tree was finished except for the Santa topper. Crystal had tried her very hardest to loosen up, but she was still hovering right on the cusp of her adult self and the little girl she kept locked up tight. I needed her to find the little girl inside her this weekend. There was no chance for a redo, and we were running out of time.

Squinting at the tree, I rubbed my temples and reviewed my plans for the next day. If a trip to the teddy-bear store and a visit with Santa hadn't done the trick, I wasn't sure that anything I had planned for tomorrow would, either.

I was starting to lose hope, and when Santa loses hope, well that's when snowballs hit the fan, because hope is kind of Santa's thing. Aside from candy canes and presents and flying reindeer, that is.

I took a deep breath and tried to reassure myself, but before I could put on a happy face, I was nailed in the back of the head by a flying object. A light one that felt suspiciously like a piece of popcorn. Grinning, I whirled around, to find her standing behind me, feigning interest in a wooden gingerbread man I had placed on the mantle.

Crossing the room, I tapped her on the shoulder, fixing my face into that of an amused but stern Daddy. "Did you throw popcorn at Daddy?"

Crystal bit her bottom lip and shook her head. There was a light in her eyes that hadn't been there a few minutes ago.

"Now you're lying to Daddy? You're being very naughty right now, little one. Do you need a spanking?"

"No." Her hands flew behind her to cover her bottom, and she shook her head emphatically from side to side.

"No, Daddy?" I coaxed. I hadn't gotten her to actually call me Daddy yet, unless she was referring to me in teasing, but we were close. She wanted to. I could almost hear her thoughts at war with one another.

She nibbled her lip and blinked up at me but didn't take the bait. Instead, she picked up another piece of popcorn and flicked it at me. "Ooh, you're in for it now," I laughed, lunging toward her.

She shrieked as she ran, tossing the contents of the bowl over her shoulder as she tried to get away from me. She wasn't fast enough, nor did the avalanche of popcorn create the obstacle she apparently thought it would. I caught her wrist, tossed her over my shoulder, and pinned her on her back on the couch.

"There's only one way to deal with these kinds of naughties." I rolled up the sleeves of my red flannel and kept my expression as grim as possible. She gulped, watching each measured movement I made. I took a deep breath and shook my head. "Just remember you asked for this." Then I staged a tickle attack. She wiggled with all of her might to get away, giggling and squealing the whole time.

"Uncle! Uncle! I give up!"

"Not so fast! I don't hear any magic words."

"Please!" she screeched breathlessly between gales of laughter.

"Close, but not quite what I'm looking for." I wiggled my eyebrows at her and smiled, pinning her hands above her head. Her expression changed to one of amused annoyance. She knew she was stuck. I had her right where I wanted her, and she liked it.

"Okay, okay! Daddy, Daddy, Daddy! Please stop."

"Well, since you asked nicely," I teased, loosening my hold without letting go. She reared up till her face was inches away from mine. I could smell the cocoa on her breath, and a handful of candy canes had tinted her lips to a bright red. She looked flushed, and her eyes were dilated with arousal. We were close enough to kiss, and God, but I wanted to.

Inhaling deeply, I pushed my body off hers and stood, offering her my hand. There would be time for kissing once the weekend was over. Provided I didn't muck everything up between now and then.

"Ready to add the finishing touch?" I asked, gesturing toward the tree. Dismay flickered in her eyes for a moment, but she quickly pushed it aside and nodded eagerly, reaching for the Santa topper in my hand. She looked adorable rising on tiptoe to add the final decoration, and I wanted to scoop her up and toss her into bed. And join her there. One more day, I reminded myself silently, as she came to stand next to me with her hands on her hips.

"You know, it's not so bad-looking all put together. I kinda like the piney smell, too."

I wrapped my arm over her shoulder and hugged her close. "So, little elf, what you're saying is that Daddy was right?"

"Oh geez, don't get a big head or anything." She nudged me with her elbow and rolled her eyes. Luckily, I didn't have a rule about eye rolling, or this minx would never sit again.

"The First Noel" began playing on the stereo and I turned Crystal to face me.

"May I have this dance?" I bowed, extending my hand for her to take. Crystal giggled and laid her hand in mine.

"I guess you can, but I'm not sure you deserve it. You're kind of mean with the no coffee, and the spanking, and all the rules."

She was teasing, and I chuckled. "You are so sassy."

"I can't help it. I have this urge to just… I don't know how to explain it."

"Buck the system?" I suggested.

"Yes! Like I don't want to care about anything! I want to act out, not follow the rules, not worry about expectations. Is that weird?"

"Not at all, little elf. That means you are beginning to trust me and yourself. It's exactly what I want from you. I want you to feel that childlike freedom and to experience Christmas in the way you should have when you were a child."

She nodded and laid her head on my shoulder, pressing her body against mine as we moved in time with the music. "I think it's working."

Her quiet admission elated me. It was what I had been hoping and waiting for. Now I just had to make sure she stayed in this headspace and didn't go backward or in and out like she had been all day. We danced through the song in silence, and when it ended, I spun her in a circle and dipped her with a dramatic flourish.

Once upright again, she smiled through a big yawn. "That was fun."

"Yes, it was, and now it is time for bed."

"I'm not tired," she protested. "I want to have more hot chocolate and watch another movie."

"There's always tomorrow, little one."

"Then it will be over," she pouted.

I understood her unspoken worry and mentally mirrored it with my own. "It doesn't have to be. Let's see how tomorrow goes and then we can figure out the rest, okay?"

"But I still don't want to go to bed."

"It's cute that you think you have a choice, little elf. It's well past nine, and I've kept you up late enough already. Little girls need sufficient sleep."

"Nine! Are you kidding me? I never go to bed before eleven," she argued, despite the fact exhaustion was evident in every line of her face and the sag of her shoulders.

"Not tonight. Let's go." Not entertaining argument, I turned her toward her room and sent her off with a smack to her perfect backside.

"Ow," she whined, rubbing the spot. "You don't have to be so rough!"

"There's more where that came from if you are not ready for bed in fifteen minutes."

"Fine." She drew out the word with exaggerated exasperation.

"I'm sure you mean 'yes, Daddy'?" I quirked a brow at her, and she stuck her tongue out at me. "That's not very respectful, little girl."

"Well, I'm not feeling very respectful. You're being mean, and it's not fair!"

I raised my eyebrows and refrained from stealing her favorite move, the eye roll.

"You'd better start feeling it, little elf. Little girls who are rude and disrespectful to their Daddies end up feeling very sorry for themselves when they are sleeping on their tummies with a hot bottom."

She scowled, and with my mind-reading abilities turned on, I could hear her mental struggle as she pondered how far to push me, and if the risk would be worth the reward, or whether she might like the consequences of pushing too far. It was a very enlightening conversation she was having with herself, and it let me know that no matter what happened, I had to stay firm in my resolve. Daddies did not like to be tested.

The war played out for several minutes, and finally, she

turned and headed for her room, arms crossed over her chest and feet heavy as she stomped down the hall. "Whatever," she mumbled.

I was elated that she was getting comfortable enough to push, but I was a Daddy, and she was about to find out exactly what happened to little girls who poked the bear. She hadn't been that naughty, but I had made threats, and they must be followed through.

"Crystal Angelina Turner, get your little butt back here right now, and try that again, with less attitude this time." She froze, but did not turn to obey. "If I have to count to three, you will be getting extra with the wooden spoon, little girl." That got her. Eyes wide, she turned to stare at me open-mouthed over her shoulder. I pointed to a spot in front of me and waited, adopting the stance of an impatient Daddy. "Now, please."

She turned, but didn't take any steps to move toward me. "I don't want a spanking."

"That's funny because you seem to be begging for one. Come here."

It was going to be a standoff. That was evident when she propped her hands on her hips and jutted out her chin, meeting my firm stare with a smoldering glare. "I don't want to."

"One." My hand came to rest on my thick leather belt. I wouldn't use it on her, but she didn't know that.

"Stop counting!" she whined, deflating from her earlier defiance. "I'll be good and get ready for bed. I really am tired." She started down the hall to her room.

"Two," I continued. "It's too late to obey now, little one. You made your bed, and now you have to lie in it. On your tummy. After you take the spanking you have coming."

She turned but stayed rooted in place.

"You do not want me to get to three. I suggest you obey."

Finally accepting her impending doom, she dropped her chin to her chest and shuffled toward me, slowly. With her cute little pout and defeated stance, she actually looked more like a naughty six-year-old, than a thirty-one-year-old woman, if only for that brief moment.

"I'm nothing if not patient, little elf," I said as she shuffled toward me at a snail's pace. "I don't care if it takes you all night to get here. All you are doing is delaying the inevitable and making me want to forgo my hand altogether and wear you out with my trusty wooden spoon."

Heeding my warning, she picked up her pace, quickly coming to a stop in front of me. She took a deep breath and clasped both hands in front of her, staring down at them.

Hooking my finger under her chin, I raised her face until her gaze met mine. "Daddy doesn't like that kind of testy and rude behavior, little girl."

She gave a soft moaning whine and nibbled her lip. "Sorry?" It came out like a question.

"Are you?"

She shrugged. "If I am, will you not spank me?"

"It's a little late for that. You had several chances, and you continued to do whatever you could to make it worse for yourself. Now, do you want to tell me what's going on in that little head of yours? When little girls test their Daddies like that, there is usually an underlying reason."

"I'm not tired. I never go to bed this early, and it's been a fun day. I don't want it to end yet."

Pure exhaustion radiated off of her body, and I knew it was partly responsible for her little state of mind and her testy behavior. I wasn't complaining, but I was going to do what had to be done. "I'm pretty sure you are beyond exhausted, and you are telling fibs right now, but that's okay. Even if I am wrong, you will be nice and tired when I'm done with you. For the record, though, I did not tell you to go to bed. I told you to get ready for bed. There's one more thing on the agenda for tonight." *Well, two now,* I mused.

"Oh. Oops."

Shaking my head, I held my hand out to her. "Come on. Let's get this over with."

"You don't have to spank me! You should have told me the plan. This isn't my fault, it's yours," she argued desperately but placed her hand in mine and allowed me to lead her down the hall to her bedroom.

"That's interesting logic, but you might want to reconsider that kind of behavior justification. It won't end well for you. Your time and energy would be better spent searching for any shred of remorse you have for your attitude and disobedience."

She stayed quiet and didn't resist me at all as I sat down on the bed and flipped her over my knee.

I sat and listened. Her mind was racing with all sorts of things she wanted to say. Some were remorseful, others flippant, and some were self-deprecating and angry, but she couldn't settle on any one thing. I gave her a minute to think before I pushed her further by hooking my thumbs into the waistband of her leggings and lowering her pants. Her hands flew backward, and she squealed.

"Wait! Wait, wait! What are you doing?"

"Well, that's a silly question, little elf."

"But, this isn't right. You didn't do it this way this morning!"

"Oh, you mean because I spanked you over your jammies first this morning? Well, I hate to break it to you, but not all spankings are created equal. That was your first one, and I was being nice. But you were given a lot of chances tonight, little one, and yet here we are. So, we will begin on the bare this time." I grabbed her wrists and held them in my hand, pinning them to the small of her back, out of my way.

"Maybe it will make a more lasting impression." I looked over her backside, examining it for any remnants from this morning's spanking, but as I had expected, there were none. I had a fresh canvas to paint. I rubbed my hand over her milky-white skin, and goose bumps rose on her flesh.

"Please don't spank me," she whimpered weakly, but with her hands pinned, there was no fight. She lay limply over my knee and waited.

"Do you have anything to say for yourself before I begin?"

She shook her head, but I could hear her thoughts. She was yelling at herself to say something, but stayed silent until the first smack.

"Ow! Shit! No, no, no!" She scrambled to get away, but I didn't let her gain an inch, laying down five more swats before I addressed her.

"You will watch your mouth, or I will stick a bar of soap in it. Do you understand me?"

I peppered her with six more swats to make my point before she could answer. She protested and squirmed.

"Okay, okay, I'm sorry! I understand. Stop!"

"We haven't even started yet, little elf. I am very disappointed in your behavior, and you are going to be a very thoroughly chastised little girl once we are finished here."

"But you made your point!" she hollered, squirming as if I was actually going to let her get loose of my grasp. "I get it! I'm sorry. I promise! I'll be nice, and I'll obey!"

"I don't think you do get it. If you did, you would know you aren't in control here, little one. There is nothing you can do or say to make me stop before I'm ready. And you are not even close to how sorry you need to be."

I started spanking again, this time concentrating a few swats at a time to the same spot before moving on to the next. She kicked her feet and arched her back, trying to gain some leverage to get away. "You aren't going anywhere, little elf. Maybe you should concentrate your efforts elsewhere. Like perhaps on formulating a proper apology."

"I can't concentrate on anything with you hitting me!"

"I am not hitting you. I am spanking your naughty bottom." I stopped for a minute, giving her a chance to catch her breath before starting again with renewed vigor. This time I had the promised and dreaded spoon.

Taking a moment to admire the slender bamboo spoon I had found among her kitchen utensils, I smacked it hard against her sit spots, first on one side and then the other. And then I waited for the protests that I knew would come.

"Ow! Ow! Ow! What in the ever-loving…?" She turned to glare over her shoulder, her mouth dropping when she saw the offending implement. "Nooo! Not fair! Your hand hurts enough!"

"I told you that if you did not obey, I would be using the spoon. A Daddy always does what he says."

She groaned and kicked her feet but did not argue any further. Instead, she turned away, hung her head, and braced herself for what was coming.

This spanking wasn't really about disrespect or bratting, and I suspect she knew that, whether she was willing to admit it or not.

It was about giving in to that little girl inside her. I couldn't really blame her for bratting, and I guess part of me had wanted her to do it because I knew what the end result would be. I wasn't sure how I had become such an expert on Littles and Daddy Doms, but it was another job perk. I just seemed to know the things I needed to know. And I knew a meeting with the dreaded wooden spoon would do the trick. A spoon was like a Little's kryptonite. The implement they loved to hate, and the one that brought them crashing into little space, and when wielded correctly, kept them there.

That's the result I was hoping for, and I didn't plan on stopping until I achieved it. Crystal was stubborn as all get-out, but she was also tired and hovering right on the cusp of giving in completely. It shouldn't take long to reduce her to the sweet six-year-old I knew lived inside her.

Determined to prove my point, I picked up the pace and the power in my swing. The wooden spoon cracked against the pinkened skin without pattern or mercy, again and again.

She squirmed and cried out, and gasped for air between the swats, which were falling hard and fast against the fleshy center of her rounded cheeks. I loved every peep she made, and the way she squirmed against my lap had me hard and aching with need, but I didn't let on.

I heard her soft gasp when the dam of tears broke, and she finally let loose. I slowed but didn't stop.

"Stop," she whimpered. "Please stop."

I could tell the cries were coming from a place deep within her, beyond her control. She was growing desperate, saying whatever she could to stop the spanking from continuing. But she wasn't done yet.

"I will not stop," I informed her, firmly cracking the spoon hard against the crease between her bottom and thighs. The sit spots. *That ought to do it.* "I will keep going until I am certain that my little girl has been thoroughly chastised for her testing and naughty behavior and has fully received the message that her Daddy does what he says."

"I get it! I do!" she sniveled, writhing against me.

I stilled the spoon for a second, creating a false sense of security before letting go with a fresh barrage of swats, first on the left cheek and then on the right. "I don't think you do."

"I do! I do! I do! I'm sorry! I promise! I won't test you anymore, and I know when you say something you mean business, and I'll try my best to obey and enjoy!"

"Good girl," I murmured, continuing my onslaught. There was one more word I wanted to hear break from those pretty little lips before I could rest assured that my mission had hit its mark.

"Please, Daddy!" she gasped, when I moved my attention back to her sit spots. "Please, Daddy. I'm sorry! I'll be a good girl. I promise."

I slowly eased my tempo, bringing the swats down in strength and quickness while I listened to her cry out apologies and promises between quiet gasping sobs.

When her cries fell silent so did my spoon.

Her bottom was red and hot to the touch. I pulled her panties and leggings up and lifted her into my lap, holding her tight as I waited for her tears to subside. Cleaning her face with a handkerchief, I kissed her forehead.

"You're a good girl, little elf."

"Then w-why did you s-spank me?"

I stood her in front of me so that I could see her face. Using the pad of my thumbs, I wiped away the last few tears that had escaped. "Because even good girls need reminders that their Daddies are going to hold them to a certain standard. Daddies have to be strong and unrelenting. Trust me, I would much rather spoil you than spank you, little one, but unfortunately, with me, you can't have one without the other. Come on, I'll help you get dressed for bed."

"I can do it." Her face was a mask of uncertainty, like she wanted me to help, but didn't want to give in that fully.

"I want to take care of you. Will you let me help you, please?" I posed it as a question on purpose because I wanted her to know it was her choice. If she did not want me to see her in a state of undress in this stage of our relationship, I would fully understand.

She shifted from foot to foot, and for the first time ever I felt like I was invading her privacy by listening to her thoughts so I stopped.

"I guess if you want to," she whispered.

"Thank you, little elf."

I snapped a Christmas nightgown into my hands, and she giggled. It was green and had smiling Christmas trees all over.

"That is ridiculous."

"I know, and you will look ridiculously cute wearing it. Arms up."

She obediently raised her arms straight over her head, and I swept her shirt up and off her body. I tried to avert my eyes, and not notice the curves of her hips or the swell of her breasts, but I was no saint. *I am going to need a cold shower once she is in bed for the night*, I thought, rushing to shimmy the nightgown I had chosen over her head.

"There, all nice and cozy," I said, as I straightened it. Go brush your teeth and get ready for bed, and I will get ready to read you a bedtime story."

"A bedtime story? Really? My mom used to read to me every night, but that stopped when I was like six."

"Well, you are six this weekend, aren't you?"

"Oh, right." She giggled a little and smiled. "It's just weird, that's all."

"It's not weird at all. Now, go get ready for bed."

As soon as she left the room, I snapped my fingers and changed into my own pajamas and pulled back her covers. By the time I got myself comfortable in the bed, she was emerging from the bathroom with a look of contentment on her face.

"You look like you belong there."

"I feel like I belong here. Not necessarily here in this bed, but with you, wherever that may be." I patted the bed next to me. "I have my favorite Christmas book of all time here, ready for us to read. You, my little elf, are in for a treat."

She climbed into the bed, and I covered her up, making sure to tuck in the sides so that she was nice and snug.

I picked up the book and started to read. "*'Twas the night before Christmas…*"

"Hey I know this one!" she announced excitedly.

"Well good, but this is the special Santa version that my great-grandfather wrote, so listen closely." I continued reading. The book was close to the original poem with a few of the words changed to make it readable from Santa's perspective.

Crystal laid her head on my shoulder and listened intently, giggling when I exaggerated the Santa parts, especially when I ho-ho-hoed loudly.

"The end." I closed the book and kissed the top of her head. "How are you feeling, little one?"

"I think I'm tired now." She yawned as she said it, and her eyelids drooped.

"Oh good." I started to stand and tiptoe from the room, but she grabbed my arm before I could leave the bed.

"Do you really go down people's chimneys?"

"I will."

"With a giant sack of toys?"

"I don't know about giant, but yes, I will carry a sack."

"Wait, what do you mean 'will'? You've never done it before?"

"Nope. This Christmas will be my first run as Santa, hopefully."

"Hopefully?"

"Sleep, little elf. You can ask all the questions you want tomorrow." Once again, I rose from her bed and tucked the blanket around her, calling Dixie up to cuddle.

Crystal's eyes were already half-closed when the fluffy dog

climbed up to settle at her feet. Taking a moment to breathe in the picture she made, I leaned in and gave her a gentle kiss, lingering for a moment longer than necessary. This woman was to be my wife, and I wasn't sure exactly when I'd started to fall in love with her, but in this moment, when I looked at her, I knew I was looking at my future. I was head over heels.

I shut off her side-table lamp and quietly padded toward the door, but before I left her room, I remembered one last thing.

"Little elf?" I asked quietly, in case she had already nodded off to dreamland.

"Hmm?" she responded sleepily.

"What did you whisper in Mall Santa's ear? What did you ask him for?"

A sweet smile illuminated her features, barely visible in the darkness. She rolled onto her side, turning her back to me, and grabbed her new Santa bear from the edge of the bed, pulling him into her arms. I thought she wouldn't answer, and I turned to leave. I had one hand on the doorknob when her soft, sleepy voice filled the room.

"I told him that all I wanted for Christmas was you."

Tears filled my eyes. "That's all I want, too, little elf," I whispered.

8
Crystal
December 14th, 2018

I woke up the next morning feeling lighter and freer than I ever remember feeling. I was very surprised to find that my bottom was still a bit sore and tender to the touch as I shifted in bed, but the memory of the spanking put a smile on my face. Yawning, I sat up and stretched, wondering what the day had in store. Yesterday had been full of surprises, and I found myself excited to see what my Santa Daddy would come up with next. I quickly dressed and pulled my hair into a ponytail. The smell of cinnamon permeated the air, and I let my nose and growling stomach lead me to the source.

"Oh my God. I'm going to weigh a thousand pounds if you keep feeding me like this," I groaned when I caught sight of the heaping tray of fresh cinnamon rolls.

Santa smiled. "You could use a little meat on those bones."

I shook my head, wondering how early he had risen to bake, or if he had conjured these up with a snap of his fingers. "Do you even sleep?"

"Sure I do. I don't need many hours, especially this time of year when there is so much to be done. Did you sleep well, little elf?"

I felt a pang of guilt that I was keeping him from his work, but then I reminded myself that the weekend was his idea not mine.

"My father is overseeing my duties right now, little elf. It's tradition for the first year."

"Get out of my head," I muttered, sitting down at the table.

"I can't help it." Santa chuckled. "Your brain is an interesting place to be."

"Didn't your mom ever tell you it was rude to spy on people like that? It's a total invasion of privacy." I was half kidding. I mean, it was kind of strange to think he heard every one of my innermost thoughts, but what could I do about it?

He chuckled, and I belatedly realized that every time he laughed it sounded more like "ho ho ho." It was unreal. "No, she hasn't had the chance. It's kind of a new thing, a perk to the Santa gig," he said with a wink, setting a frosted cinnamon bun on a snowflake-shaped plate in front of me. He followed it with a huge mug of cocoa, complete with a small mountain of whipped cream and red and green sprinkles. Setting it down, he kissed the top of my head.

"Good morning. You didn't answer my question. How was your night?"

"Surprisingly restful. This looks delicious."

"Fresh from my mother's oven. I can't take credit for this one."

"I thought 'real Daddies do things the hard way'?" I lowered the tone of my voice, trying to mimic his baritone timbre.

"Ha ha, very funny. Me and baking don't mix. That's one of the many reasons I need a Mrs. Claus. But I'm still working on that, so I called for backup."

"Wait! Your mother is here?" I screeched and looked around in a panic, completely ignoring his Mrs. Claus reference. This weekend so far had been amazing, but I wasn't ready to think that far ahead.

"No, silly girl. I teleported the cinnamon buns in. This

weekend is about us. There will be plenty of time for you to meet my parents."

I chose to ignore that statement and took a generous bite of the yummy breakfast treat. It was as amazing as its scent promised it to be. The cinnamon was prominent but not overpowering, and the inside was baked to perfection. The pastry all but melted in my mouth, and don't even get me started on the frosting. It was so tasty that I used my finger to get every tiny bite off my plate.

"Oh my goodness! I think that might be the best thing I've ever eaten. Thank you." *Daddy.* It was on the tip of my tongue, but it just stuck there. It had been much easier last night after I got spanked. *What the hell?*

"You're welcome, little elf. Would you like another? We have plenty."

I shouldn't. I really shouldn't, but dammit, I did want another one. "Yes, please."

"Good girl." The huge smile on his face gave away the fact that he heard my inner argument. Why did that not feel weird anymore? Weirder still was the warmth spreading through my body at his childlike endearment.

I sipped my cocoa and groaned, wishing it were coffee. This was way too many feelings to deal with without caffeine. Time to drown the feelings in frosting. I dug in to my second cinnamon roll.

"Want to guess what you and Daddy will be doing today, little one?"

"Christmas," I spoke around a bite of pastry.

He laughed. "Yes, sassy pants, but what to do with Christmas?"

"How should I know? You're the expert, not me." I couldn't keep the sarcasm out of my voice. It was a defense mechanism I employed when I felt vulnerable. And Santa had me feeling hella vulnerable. When he quirked a brow at my response, I sank in my seat. I recognized that look from last night. Right before I got spanked.

"Want to try that one again? Or would you like a little attitude adjustment to begin the day?"

I shook my head. I did not want another spanking like that anytime soon. No way, no how. I was barely able to swallow the last piece of my cinnamon bun past the lump that had formed in my throat. "Sorry."

"Thank you." He winked at me, and I couldn't help but wiggle in my seat. I needed distance from him, and I needed it now.

I jumped out of my chair. "I really need a shower, umm…" Did I need to ask permission to shower? Was that a thing? This being six stuff was hard, but I definitely didn't feel all of my thirty-one years, either. I decided to err on the side of caution. "Is there time in the plan for that?"

"If you feel like you need a shower, go right ahead and have a shower. If you're doing it to avoid me, however…"

He let the threat linger, and I dropped my shoulders and sat back down.

"This is not supposed to be torture, little one. I'm excited about our day together, and I wanted to share that with you, that's all."

Guilt consumed me as I realized I was making a big deal over nothing. I was so damned confused and twisted around inside, I didn't know which way was up.

He scooted his chair away from the table and patted his knee. "Come here."

"What?" I shrieked, my heart pounding as I mentally retraced my steps. What had I done? What had I said? "Why? I apologized. I didn't do anything to earn a spanking."

"Calm down. I'm not going to spank you. I just want a cuddle."

Geez, did I feel stupid. Before I could put my foot down

my throat any further, I stood and went to him. As soon as I was close enough, he reached for my hand, pulled me to sit on his lap, and hugged me.

"I'm sorry you are so frustrated right now. I want you to do something for me, okay?"

I rested my head on his chest and nodded.

"Good girl. Close your eyes and take a nice deep breath. Think back to yesterday. Think about how it felt when you relaxed and let yourself just be." I obeyed and pulled as much air into my lungs as I could before letting it out slowly. It did feel good when I was dressing the bears and when we decorated the tree and had the popcorn fight. It had been a fun day. I smiled as he rubbed one hand up and down my back. "Good girl. Now I want you to think about the spanking and how it felt to give over that kind of complete control."

I squeezed my eyes tight. This was a little harder. That spanking had hurt. Still hurt. "Don't think about the pain, little elf. Focus on the feelings in here, not here." He tapped my head and then pinched my ass, and I squeaked in surprise.

"Ow, meanie." I rubbed the spot and tried to get up, but he held on.

"Nope, you aren't going anywhere. We are not finished here quite yet."

I sighed and stilled, knowing if he wasn't ready to let me up, I wasn't getting up.

"I want you to try something for me today. Can you do that?"

"Depends what it is, I guess." I eyed him skeptically.

"I want you to call me Daddy, all day. Whenever you address me, I want to hear you say it. It will help you let go."

"You're joking, right? I can't call you...that." I swallowed hard. I was thinking it constantly, but saying it was so much harder.

"You did last night, more than once."

"That was after… you know."

"After I spanked you for being a naughty little girl? Yes it was, and if you need that kind of incentive again, I can provide it, but I don't think you want another big spanking, do you, little elf?"

I shook my head. I absolutely did not want another spanking like that. I could still feel that one.

"Words, little one."

I bit my lips and stayed quiet. I honestly didn't think I could do it. The idea of it was so foreign, and I was scared. What if all of this was some crazy stunt to get me to believe and then he walked away?

"Trust your Daddy."

"I can't say it," I admitted.

He didn't say another word, and before I knew it, I was facedown on his lap once again.

"No, no, no. Please don't!"

He skimmed my pants and panties down, and the cool air heightened my nerves. I craned my neck to look back at him.

"If you can't let go, then I will help you, simple as that." He lifted his hand, and I braced myself.

Just say it, I pleaded with my own stubbornness as frustrated tears pricked the back of my eyes. *You want to say it! Say it.*

His hand fell rapidly three times on each cheek, and that's all it took.

"Please, Daddy. Please, don't spank me! I will do what you said. I'll trust you. I'm sorry. Please don't spank me anymore."

"Good girl. That wasn't so hard now, was it?" He pulled my pants and panties back up and helped me stand. Taking my cheeks in his hands, he kissed my forehead. "I think you will be pleasantly surprised with the amount of freedom you feel today, little elf. Are you ready to have some fun?"

"Yes, D-daddy." I choked on the word, but breathed a sigh of relief once it was out. It did feel good. I nodded and wiped the unshed tears from my eyes. He was my Daddy, at least for the rest of the day, and he would take care of me. That much I could trust.

Each time I called him Daddy, it felt better and better on my lips. It was as if a weight had been lifted off my shoulders, and I was free to enjoy life. And when Santa Daddy said there would be fun, he wasn't kidding. I emerged from dressing for the day to find two tables in my main living area. One was covered with every cookie-decorating tool imaginable, different colors of frosting, sprinkles, and edible glitter. The other held a few baking pans, large balls of dough, rolling pins, and flour. There were cookie cutters of all shapes and sizes depicting different Christmas symbols. I could already smell cookies baking.

"I got one pan in the oven already, so we don't waste any time. Are you ready for one of my favorite Christmas traditions?"

"They're all your favorite." I giggled.

"Yeah, you might be right about that. I'm kind of crazy for Christmas. Job hazard." He winked. "Oh well, come on, little elf. These cookies aren't going to decorate themselves."

I positioned myself in front of one of the large balls of dough and watched him out of the corner of my eye. I had never baked anything that didn't come out of a box, and I had no idea what I was doing. He looked up and smiled.

"Pull off a chunk of dough and flour your rolling pin then just roll it out. Watch." He demonstrated for me, expertly flattening the dough into a perfect sheet. I copied his movements, excited to find out the process was pretty simple. Upbeat Christmas music played in the background as we cut out and decorated dozens of cookies. Daddy sang most of the songs, and I found myself dancing along and joining in the chorus of some of the familiar tunes. It was so much fun, and it was over before I was ready.

"That's the last of them, little elf." He wiped his hands on the goofy apron he had been sporting all morning. "What do you think?"

"Are you sure there's not more dough? I want to do more."

"No, little one, there's no more dough, but you know those little people shapes we decorated?"

I nodded. They had been some of my favorite to do. Putting frosting faces and clothing on them had been fun.

"Well they need homes, don't you think?" His eyes twinkled with mirth as he got up and walked behind the counter.

"Homes?"

"Since we already have all of the frosting, I thought it would be fun to decorate gingerbread houses." He pulled out two preassembled little houses and brought them to the table.

"I did this at school once!" I clapped my hands excitedly, surprised when I actually felt the childlike excitement building inside me. "Don't we need candy and stuff?"

He winked again and snapped his fingers. The cookie mess disappeared, in its place a fresh tablecloth and little bowls of different types of candy. Candy canes, gumdrops, chocolate-coated candies, licorice ropes, and sprinkles in every size and shape imaginable.

"You know? I don't think other Daddies can turn messes into candy like that," I teased.

"That's only one of the perks of having a Santa Daddy."

He reached over and tickled my stomach. I jumped away, laughing.

"'Bout time we got to the perks," I teased as I picked one of the houses and retrieved the green frosting.

"Ha ha, little brat. In two days, you have gotten more Christmas than some people get all season. I would call that a perk."

"I guess it's been a little fun," I admitted grudgingly. Not wanting to wait any longer, I started decorating. I knew exactly which little boy and girl cookies were going to live in my house, and I decorated it accordingly. Red-and-green frosting, lots of candies, and some edible glitter for that extra touch. Every time I looked up, I caught Daddy watching me and smiling. I couldn't help but smile back.

When the house looked exactly the way I wanted it to, I went to get the two cookies who were going to live there. I had decorated one as Santa and one as Mrs. Claus. I found them among the massive piles of cookies currently spread throughout my kitchen and took them to the frosted house. Setting them on either side, I giggled.

"All done, Daddy," I announced.

He came over to my side of the table, wrapped an arm over my shoulder, and kissed me on the head. "It's perfect, little elf."

"It really is." I sighed, with equal parts contentment and frustration. I wasn't talking about the gingerbread house, either. I laid my head on Santa and took a deep breath to calm my crazy emotions. Why was I about to cry over a freakin' gingerbread house? What was he doing to me? Clearing my throat, I turned my attention toward his creation.

"Let's see yours." I rounded the table to look at what he had done. The action was more about distraction than curiosity. His gingerbread house was decorated meticulously with blue and gold and in front of it was a little gingerbread girl with black licorice rope hair, and what looked to be a sad attempt at a dog. I giggled. "Is that me and Dixie?"

"It sure is." He smiled proudly.

"But, where's you?"

He shrugged his shoulders. "I ran out of gingerbread people. I might have eaten a few before we got to the house decorating. They're my favorite. Now, how about some lunch and a movie?" he asked with a wink, changing the subject.

"My stomach is full." I wasn't lying, either. I'd eaten more candy and cookies in one morning than I had the entire year combined.

"You need to eat real food, little one, but I don't want to make you sick. How about a movie and then lunch instead?"

"Can I pick the movie?"

"From an approved list."

"Fiiine."

"Excuse me?"

"Sorry." I covered my mouth, remembering how much trouble I'd gotten into the night before because of my attitude.

"Try again."

I dropped my hands and clasped them in front of me. "Okay, Daddy."

"Much better, silly girl."

9
Santa

"What's up, little elf?" I asked as I stirred a pot of my famous homemade chili. We had ended up skipping lunch after too much cookie nibbling during our Christmas-movie marathon. It had been a lovely day, and Crystal had stayed in her little state of mind, calling me Daddy, and being perfectly playful and mischievous.

But as the day had worn on, I had noticed that staying in her little state seemed to be more and more of a struggle. Now, she looked positively morose.

Crystal shrugged, playing with the strings of her candy-cane-striped apron, and refusing to look at me. I leaned over and tapped her on the butt with my wooden spoon. "Little elf," I growled. "Tell Daddy what's wrong."

The little nudge did nothing to ease her sadness. If anything, it seemed to make her more upset.

Frowning when she still didn't answer, I decided not to push it. Pulling the corn muffins from the oven, I scooped up two large bowls of chili, topped them with grated cheese and sour cream, and carried them to the table with the plate of muffins.

We ate in silence, with Crystal playing with her food more than eating it. She took a few small bites, but most of the meal consisted of her pushing a chunk of corn muffin through her bowl and sighing deeply.

I was at a loss. She wasn't testing me. This wasn't bratting.

I wasn't sure what was going on, but the weekend was coming to an end, and I wasn't going to leave it like this. Scooping the last bite of chili into my mouth, I pushed my bowl away, threw my napkin on the table, and stood.

Instantly, her eyes widened, and she showed more signs of life than she had in the last hour. I walked toward her and stuck out my hand. She hesitated before taking it, but eventually she put her small hand in my larger one and allowed me to help her up.

Without a word, I led her to the couch. Sitting before her, keeping hold of her hand, I brought her to stand between my legs. "Start talking, little elf, or I will have to persuade you to do so, and I don't think you want that, do you?"

Sheepishly, she shook her head, and I pulled her into my lap. She snuggled into my embrace, burying her face into my chest, but said nothing still.

"Tell Daddy what's wrong."

I heard the whimper before the rumbled vibrations reverberated on my chest.

"I don't wanna be little anymore," she whispered, so softly I had to strain to hear her.

My heart squeezed, and I felt sick to my stomach. I had followed my instincts and mucked up everything. I might have actually sent us backward, instead of forward, and there was no time for that. I had to force myself to not get upset and to keep my voice calm.

"Oh? Why is that? I thought we were having fun. I like being your Daddy."

She pulled away and looked up at me, keeping one hand pressed flat against my chest. "I like it, too," she admitted. "And I was having fun. A lot of fun. But the weekend is almost over. I have to go back to work, and you have to go back to the North Pole or wherever it is you live, and I don't wanna still be little when you leave. It will hurt too much."

"Ahh." I breathed easier, heaving a sigh of relief. I hadn't messed up. It was separation anxiety. That sucked, of course, but looking at the big picture, it was a very good sign. "Well, I certainly can't force you to stay little, my little elf. But I'm very proud of you for letting go and having a good time. And we had a very early dinner. I don't have to go for hours yet."

Suddenly, she smiled and shifted. She was no longer curled up in my lap but straddling it, facing me. My cock sprang to life at the suggestiveness of the position, and I stifled a groan. "What are you doing, little one?"

Her expression was saucy and full of sass as she leaned in closer until we were nearly nose to nose. "I don't want to be little when you leave because I want to be big."

She fluttered her eyelashes at me, and I had to chuckle.

"Getting tired of the no-coffee rule?" I guessed.

She flipped her hair to one shoulder, rolled her eyes, and shook her head. "That was cruel and unusual, but coffee is not what I am thinking about right now."

"Oh? It isn't?"

"Nope." She shifted on my lap, for the sole purpose of gyrating against my cock, and this time I couldn't hold back the growl of aroused anticipation.

"Little elf…"

"Stop calling me that. I told you, I want to be big now." With that declaration, she grabbed my face with both hands and brought her lips down hard against mine. They were soft and sweet, and tasted faintly of peppermint with a hint of chocolate. Sweet Sugarplums. I met her lips with my own, grabbing a handful of her silky hair in my fist as I deepened the kiss.

Crystal was intoxicating, and the weekend of sexual

repression had me horny as hell. As she pushed past my lips with her tongue, I dropped her hair and grabbed her ass with both hands, lifting her into the air as I stood. I twisted our bodies so that she would land on the couch, and I all but threw her there, covering her body with mine as I lowered myself over her.

"You have to be in control, don't you," she teased, grabbing the waistband of my jeans and working the belt buckle.

"Don't worry, you'll learn to like it." I grabbed her hands and pinned them over her head, pulling her shirt over them. Her bra was a shiny red satin that created a stunning contrast against her creamy white skin. "I was contemplating taking that off, but it just so happens to be my favorite color."

"Oh, really? Well, then you should see my panties. They match."

I quickly moved my attention to her tight black leggings. "These look so good on, but something tells me they will look even better off."

She lifted her hips off the couch and allowed me to skim the stretchy black fabric over her hips, down her legs, and onto the floor, revealing, as promised, a pair of sexy red-satin panties.

"You look exquisite in red," I whispered appreciatively, running my hands over the expanse of white skin between the two pieces of fabric.

"Well, isn't that lucky," she smirked.

God. I was crazy about this woman. From her sexy smirk, to her red panties and deep into her large but wounded heart. But right now, I was thinking with my cock, and he was much more interested in what lay underneath the shiny scraps of fabric than the fabric itself.

I grabbed the waistband, hooking a finger on each side. "These are sexy as hell, but they have to go."

"I was hoping you would say that. And I feel the same way about those jeans of yours."

It was all the motivation I needed. My hands left her waist and flew to my belt, working it and the zipper of my jeans quickly. I somehow managed to rid myself of them without standing, and soon, we were clad only in matching red undergarments.

"We match," I quipped.

"No surprise there. Red is your favorite color, after all."

She shimmied down and reached for my cock, grabbing it through the thin fabric of my boxer briefs. I licked my lips and closed my eyes, unsurprised to feel the fabric sliding over my ass and down my thighs as she angled for a better grip.

When her hand found my cock, the skin-to-skin contact made my eyes roll back in my head.

"This isn't really fair, you know. You still have your panties on."

"I don't see you doing anything about it," she challenged.

"Touché." I quickly rectified the problem, removing the satin thong and slingshotting it across the room. It landed on top of Dixie, who looked up from her dog bed with bored eyes, shook off the offending object, and went back to sleep.

In the time it took me to slingshot the panties and look at the dog, Crystal had changed positions and was now knelt in front of me, eye level with my cock. And she was looking at it like a reindeer looks at a carrot stick.

I swallowed thickly. Before I could do anything else, she cupped my balls with one hand and wrapped the other around my girth, moving forward until her mouth was poised at the tip of my cock.

I inhaled deeply, anticipating the warmth of her lips around my tip, and shuddered when she smiled and took me in her mouth.

I was in bliss for two full seconds before she frowned and pulled back in surprise.

"Oh! You taste like candy canes!"

"Do I?" I chuckled. "Well, they are my favorite food group. I eat a lot of them."

"No, I mean you taste exactly like a candy cane. It's not like a hint or an essence. Your dick is practically candy coated. Like for real."

I shrugged. "I wouldn't know, but it must be a job hazard, or a perk, depending on how you feel about peppermint, I guess."

"I love it." Ending the conversation, she took me in her mouth and began to blow me with more enthusiasm than I would have dreamed possible. Folding my hands behind my head, I leaned back, thrusting my hips out so as to push myself farther into her mouth.

Her tongue traced circles up my dick as she licked and sucked to her heart's content. She was slow and thorough, savoring every inch of my candy stick. I was enjoying every moment of her exploration.

She took me deeper into her mouth until my balls were touching her chin, and I moaned in ecstasy when she increased the pressure and gave my sack a soft squeeze. I closed my eyes and threw my head back, moaning. If she didn't stop, this was going to be over before it started. Blasted peppermint dick.

I grabbed her hair with both hands and used it as leverage, slowly pulling her off me while thoroughly enjoying every second of her lips sliding down my cock. When she got to the tip, she blinked up at me with a pouty smile and wide eyes.

"Get up here," I growled, helping her to her feet by her hair. When she was standing, I grabbed her hips and pulled her body against mine, relishing the feel of her female softness against my own hard hairiness. My lips closed over hers with far less gentleness than our previous kiss. I was rough and demanding as I claimed her lips with as much ferocity as she had claimed my cock. My need for her was feral and unforgiving, a wicked side effect of the weekend's pent-up sexual tension.

I had no patience left and no desire to take things slowly, but no desire to rush things, either.

This was no hot and heavy one-night stand. If I played my cards right, this woman would be my wife, and I wanted our first time together to be special.

Panting through my arousal, I broke our kiss and pulled her body close to mine. "I think it's time to move this to the bedroom."

Her breathing was shallow as she nodded her agreement, and we could hardly keep our hands off each other as we made the short journey down the hallway to her room. We didn't bother to close the door before we stumbled over to the bed and fell onto it, side by side.

We lay there naked, staring at each other while we caught our breath. Then we inhaled simultaneously and almost head-butted into each other as we leapt forward, closing the space between us. In only a minute, we were a crazy tangle of sweaty limbs. My hands were all over her, and hers were all over me. I kissed and licked every inch of exposed skin, exploring every curve, and savoring each and every point of contact, committing it to memory. She was exquisite.

She moaned and writhed under my touch. When my lips closed over her soft mound, her moans intensified before turning to whimpers.

"Santa, please."

"Please what?"

She raked her nails up my back and grabbed at my shoulders. "Please. I want you. Your cock. Please. Now."

Just hearing her say cock had me ready to bust a chestnut, and I hurried to oblige, scooting up the bed to cover her body with mine. I started to thrust myself into her but was pleasantly surprised when she rolled over and climbed on top, straddling me. She poised her hips above me, hovering her soft pussy at the tip of my cock, teasing me until I was the one whimpering with need.

"Get your sweet little pussy on me and give me some of that sugar," I growled, reaching back to give her ass a hearty slap. She jumped, impaling herself onto my cock. I grinned.

"Now I've got you right where I want you."

"Took you long enough."

We started out slow, but soon our lovemaking reached a frenzy. It felt so good inside her, and I loved to watch her perfect breasts jiggle inside the red satin as she rode my cock like it was her job.

My hands rested on her perfect ass, grabbing hold and using her body to plunge deeper into her soft folds. She felt like heaven.

I thrust into her, watching the ecstasy on her face as we came together, and trying to stave off my own orgasm.

But she was too gorgeous, and it was too perfect, and it had been too long. I pushed the pads of my fingers into the soft flesh of her ass as I came, screaming her name.

We came simultaneously, and instead of screaming Yule, this little minx cried out, "Santa Daddy!"

If I hadn't come already, I would have then.

Crystal

"Wow," I panted, rolling over on the bed to face my naked Santa. "Well, that's one way to end the weekend."

"We still have hours yet, before I have to go." Santa leaned up on the bed, resting an elbow on the mattress and his chin on one hand. "Are you hungry, little elf? You didn't really eat dinner."

I was starving, but I didn't want him to leave my bed. I was about to say no, but the way he was peering at me twisted up my insides. In the nick of time, I remembered his stupid mind-reading skills. I sighed.

"I could eat," I admitted. "But I don't want to get up, and I don't want you to, either."

"I'll let you in on a secret, little elf," he whispered, leaning in close. "I wouldn't leave this bed right now for all the cocoa and candy canes in the world."

I giggled, suddenly feeling more six than thirty-one, and Santa snapped his fingers. I blinked and waited to see what treats he would conjure up this time. Two steaming mugs of cocoa appeared on the nightstand, and a pizza box sat on the bed between us. I clapped my hands in excitement then rolled my eyes at myself and how little I felt all of a sudden.

Santa smiled, opening the box, and grabbing up a hot slice dripping with melted cheese. He offered it to me, and I took it happily.

"Looks like I chose well."

I didn't respond. I was too busy shoving pizza into my mouth. I was suddenly famished from our activities, and I quickly inhaled that slice and a second one.

"You're not eating," I accused between mouthfuls.

"I ate *my* dinner."

"I had a different kind of hunger on my mind, I guess," I quipped, closing the pizza box and moving it off of the bed so I could lay my head on his chest.

"I guess so." He was quiet for a second, stroking my hair.

I could almost hear the wheels turning in his brain. "Did you have a good weekend, little elf? Did that help, do you think?"

I sat up suddenly, took a deep breath and stock of my feelings. I could still feel a twinge of tenderness in my ass if I shifted just right, but the rest of me felt lighter somehow, like pain had been lifted. It felt crazy to admit that. A lump formed in my throat when I even thought about voicing it. And I knew that Santa was probably reading my mind anyway. I sighed.

"I'm going to miss it all, I think. And you."

"I'm not going anywhere, little elf. Well, tonight I am, eventually. But I'll be back, and soon. We don't have much time you know."

I rolled my eyes as I did every time he made thinly veiled references to the impending doom of Christmas that he claimed would happen if I didn't agree to become his Mrs. Claus.

"You're awfully presumptuous, you know," I grumbled, hiding a smile. "And bossy."

"It's not presumption. It's destiny." He winked, taking my hand in his. "It's what is meant to be, little elf. And it may be a little crazy, and it may be a little fast, but that's only part of the magic of Christmas. You can't have a magical Christmas without a Mrs. Claus, and the love story between Santa and the Mrs.... Well, that's what builds the Christmas magic."

I scowled and pulled my hand away. "God, you're corny, you know that? You're just a big velvety ball of Christmas corniness sometimes."

"Yep. And you, my dear, are a master at changing the subject."

"What am I supposed to say? I've known you for like four days! How am I supposed to sit here and discuss a future with you? A future that involves me somehow morphing into this perfect specimen of Christmas cheer, no less? How can I possibly consider any of that without questioning my very sanity?"

"Because you know what we have is good. It may be crazy and a bit unconventional, but it's good. And the sex we had? That was more than good, little elf. It was magical."

My cheeks burned at the memory of how wild I had gotten in my pursuit of him. Him and his candy-cane-flavored dick. But it wasn't only the sex that had me hiding my face in embarrassment, it was the whole weekend and how much I had thoroughly enjoyed it all, even the little stuff.

I sat there biting my tongue, trying to stop my lips from speaking the words my brain was thinking, and finally I blurted them out. "If everything you say is true, and we are destined to be together, and I eventually become your Mrs. Claus… Could I sometimes be six again? Not like, all the time, just, ya know, sometimes." My hands still covered my face, but I peeked through my fingers and could feel my skin heating as I grew more flushed with each word I spoke.

Santa's large hands covered mine, gently pulling them down, exposing more than just my physical self to his knowing gaze. I scrunched my eyes closed.

"Open your eyes and look at me, little elf."

I opened one eye. His expression was gentle, full of compassion and mirth. "We are destined to be together," he began. "And you will be my Mrs. Claus."

I rolled my one open eye before he continued.

"And we can absolutely do it again, and soon. You still have to experience a childlike Christmas morning, you know. The experience isn't really complete without it."

My other eye opened, and I breathed a sigh of relief at his kind and encouraging words. At least one of us didn't think the other one was crazy.

"I'm the good kind of crazy," Yule interjected, reading my mind again.

"If you say so."

"I do. Now get over here and give me a kiss. I have to leave soon."

10
Santa

"Ho, ho, ho!" I walked down the aisles of the toy workshop, watching the elves man the conveyor belts. They could build an average of a toy a minute, but even with a hundred elves, we put in long days.

"Looking good, Elmer."

"Great work, Amelia."

"Nice truck, Bobby!"

Each elf I addressed beamed up at me for a second before returning their attention to their work. The elves took toymaking very seriously. More so than any of the rest of their jobs, and there were a lot of jobs to do. It took a lot to keep the North Pole running smoothly.

I had a ton of work to do, but these were my morning rounds, important for keeping up morale. And I needed the distraction. Alone in my office, I couldn't keep my mind from wandering to Crystal, her red satin bra, and the taste of her lips.

And I was doing it again. Great jumping jelly beans.

The bell rang, signaling the first cocoa break of the morning, and I retired to my office and poured myself a fresh cup of cocoa, which I seriously considered spiking.

I needed to see her. I could hardly focus on my work, and I had no idea what I was supposed to be doing. With a sigh, I cracked open the book that held the naughty list and stared at her name.

Crystal Angelina Turner. Even her name was sexy. I rubbed my face with my hands. *Focus, Yule!*

"So, when do your mother and I get to meet her?"

"Arrgh!" I jumped at the sound of my father's voice, spilling my cocoa in my lap. *Kringle Krisps! I am totally spiking the next mug.* "Dad! You have got to stop doing that!"

My father laughed and handed me a napkin from the cocoa cart to wipe up the spill.

"I'm not trying to scare you. Focus, Son. Pay attention to your surroundings. Get your head out of the clouds."

I glared at him. "What do you want?"

"That's obvious. We want to meet her. Your fiancée. The future of Christmas. Your Mrs. Claus."

"She's not my fiancée yet, Dad. Got a ways to go on that front."

"Might want to speed up the process." My father pointed to the calendar on the wall. "You have one week until Christmas Eve, Son. It's go time."

I scowled. "I'm aware of the date. I've been working very hard to balance my job with my mission. You are the one who gave me only two weeks to pull off a near-impossible task."

"It's tradition that you become Santa on the eve of your thirty-ninth birthday, and you have the remainder of the time between your birthday and Christmas to find and marry your Mrs. Claus. That's not my fault. It's the way it has always been."

"Yeah, yeah, yeah. Well, maybe you should have had me in January or March, then, instead of two weeks before Christmas."

My father shrugged. "You were a St. Patty's day present, Son. What can I say? You know it's my second favorite holiday."

The reference to my conception was more than I could

take right now. "Get out of my office. I have a ton of work to do, no thanks to you."

"Whatever you say. Just bring her here this weekend. You mother needs at least two days to plan a proper wedding." He snapped his fingers and was gone.

Thank God.

Crystal

I kept the decorations up. Every single one of them, and when I looked at them, I smiled. My ass clenched, and my pussy tingled every time I caught a glimpse of that ridiculous Santa tree topper, or the silly gingerbread houses I didn't have the heart to throw away. Not to mention the small pile of wrapped packages under the tree that grew larger each day. Every morning, when I woke up, there were at least two new ones. And then, of course, there was his parting gift. A huge centerpiece vase on the dining table filled to the brim with candy canes. At least, it had been filled to the brim when he left Sunday night. It was now Wednesday, and my supply was dwindling. I couldn't get enough of the sweet minty sticks, and every time I put one in my mouth, I thought of Yule slamming me against the wall and taking me like his own naughty little elf.

Stupid nickname. I missed it, and him. I missed the ridiculous way he hummed Christmas songs under his breath constantly and the way he drank cocoa with every meal. I missed the never-ending supply of corny Christmas pajamas he snapped into existence.

I hadn't heard from him since Sunday night, but that was no surprise. Christmas was only eight days away. He had a plethora of Santa Claus duties to tend to and far more important things to do than indulge the repressed dreams of a confirmed anti-Christmasite on the naughty list.

"The naughty list thing is a problem, but imagine my joy when I opened my nonbeliever list today and watched your name fade right off the page."

His deep voice echoed behind me, and I turned to see him standing there, all gorgeous six foot one of him, clothed in his uniform of red velvet.

"Yule!" I scolded, calling him by his real name, "Don't do that! Can't you teleport to outside the front door or something halfway normal?" I shrieked, even as my insides melted at the sight of him.

He shrugged and snagged a candy cane from the vase. "The magic isn't perfect. I think of you and then I teleport to wherever you are. Lucky for us, you weren't in the bathroom."

Annoyed by the thought of such a gross privacy invasion, I scowled at him.

He just stood there, casually unwrapping the candy cane before sticking it into his mouth with a suggestive grin. "I missed you, little elf."

My shoulders sagged as the week's stress seemed to roll off my body in waves with those five simple words. I walked toward him and all but fell into his arms. His red jacket was soft and warm and smelled like pine and peppermint. He held me for several minutes before taking me by the shoulders and pulling me back to hold me at arm's length. He grabbed my chin with the crook of one finger and lifted my face until my gaze met his. The miniature candy cane stuck out from the corner of his mouth, reminding me of our last night together and giving me all kinds of naughty thoughts.

"Do you really believe, little elf?" His face held a mixture of hope and skepticism.

"Well, your magical book of secrets says I do," I joked, "so I must. Besides, it's kind of hard not to with you teleporting in here with your mind reading, and your perfect gifts, and your freaking magical flying sleigh."

Crunching the candy cane between his teeth, he quickly swallowed. "God, that is so fruitcaking hot."

He grabbed the base of my neck and backed me against the wall with lust on his face and passion in his eyes. He kissed me with a deepness and longing that filled my soul and sent only one message. This man wanted me.

Damn. Who would have thought it would be believing in Santa that made me irresistible?

The fervor with which he kissed me and the pure unbridled desire he held for me fueled my own need. I was frantic in my mission to relieve him of his bulky uniform. The Santa suit was cute, but Santa himself was sexy as sin.

I wrestled with his jacket, and yanked at the large metal belt buckle.

Yule tossed his head back and laughed. "Little elf," he said, snapping his fingers. "If you wanted my clothes off, all you had to do was ask."

He magically removed not only his own clothes, but all of mine as well. Holy shit.

He was naked perfection, standing there with his rock-hard erection and self-satisfied smirk. I threw myself onto him, wrapping my legs around his waist. He stumbled backward, taking us to my couch, collapsing into a sitting position with me straddling him, my legs still wrapped behind his back. I felt his erection press against my opening, and I spasmed with frantic need, hoisting myself onto him, impaling myself with his candy stick.

Where our first lovemaking session had been slower and

sweeter, as we explored each other's bodies, this one was hot, heavy, and reckless with abandon as we took what we needed from one another, grinding together with a passionate heat. We had one goal. Release, and I was hovering on the brink.

"Call me Daddy," Santa growled, plunging his cock so far into me I felt my insides shift.

"Jingle balls, Yule!" I growled back, riding his cock like it was a wave, and I was a surfer.

"You know you want to. Do it." He was commanding it, and his authoritative tone made my pussy spasm.

"Daddy." I whispered it reverently, shocked at how good it felt.

"Say it again." He grabbed my breasts, cupping them while he tweaked my nipples ever so lightly.

I gasped in pain. Sweet, sensual pain. My body seemed to heat from the inside out, and light exploded behind my eyes. I saw stars.

"Santa Daddy!" I cried it out as I screamed my release, watching his eyes dilate as he, too, orgasmed, filling me with his cum.

"Oh God!" I jumped off him quickly, taking his dick in my mouth and swallowing the juices of his arousal. I wasn't on birth control, and we hadn't thought to use a condom, as it had all happened so fast.

His cum was thick but sweet. I licked my lips, searching the banks of my memory for the familiar taste.

Fucking eggnog. His jizz tastes like fucking eggnog. Because, of course it did. I licked every last drop from his tip, enjoying teasing him with my tongue as he spasmed inside my mouth.

Finally, I released him, closing my eyes as I collapsed onto the couch beside him with my head in his naked lap.

"Oh God," I moaned, covering my face with my hands. I could still taste the hints of peppermint and eggnog. "This is crazy. It's crazy what you do to me. I'm falling for you, Yule. I'm freaking falling for Santa Yule Claus! What the h-e-double candy canes is wrong with me? This is insane." *So is the fact that I can no longer cuss without substituting crazy Christmas words in place of normal adult curse words.*

"It's not insane. I've seen insane, and this is not it. It might be a little crazy, but crazy doesn't have to be a bad thing. Sometimes, a little bit of crazy is just what we need in our lives, little elf, and what I need is you. Crazy or not, I need you."

I didn't respond, as I lay there, still trying to catch my breath from our sexual escapades.

Yule moaned underneath me, leaning down to lay a kiss upon my lips. "Little elf, there is nothing I would like more than to be here with you all night, but alas, I have work to do, and you have work in the morning. You need a good night's sleep, and I have hours left in my workday. I hate to screw and run, but I had to see you."

My face fell, my lips pursed into a pout, and I felt the sting of tears behind my eyes. I already felt his absence, and he wasn't even gone yet.

After getting his suit back on, Santa gathered me into his arms and stood. He carried me into my bedroom where he made another pair of ridiculous Christmas pajamas appear in thin air and then onto my body. Pink covered with poodles and candy canes. With matching socks. It was impossible not to smile as I looked down at my ridiculous getup.

Yule took my hand and led me to bed, tucking me in, and lying down next to me. I was under the covers, and he was over them.

He took my hand in his and held it. I was glad he was with me still, not doing a complete "screw and run" as he called it. And yet, I knew he had work to do.

I sighed. "Thank you for coming over," I whispered. "I

missed you. I didn't know when I was going to see
you again."

"This weekend," Yule responded confidently. "I'll see you
Friday night. And I'll try to use the doorbell this time. By the
way, dress for cold weather. We're going to the North Pole.
My parents can't wait to meet you."

Before I could ask questions, or, God forbid, get his
phone number, he leaned forward, kissed my forehead,
touched his nose, gave a wink, and was gone.

Gosh dang merry fruitcaking teleporting Santa.

Santa
December 19th, 2018

I didn't use the doorbell, but it wasn't for lack of trying. Her
pull was too strong, and my thoughts were too focused. I
wanted to be with her, and that's where I appeared. Wherever
she was.

This time it happened to be her bedroom. She was sitting
on her bed, surrounded by piles of clothing and an open suit-
case. Her face was morphed into an intense frown, and she
was so lost in thought, she didn't even seem to notice my
arrival.

"Little elf, you're not packed," I spoke quietly, so as not
to scare her.

When she looked up, there were tears in her eyes.

I quickly crossed the room to sit next to her on the edge
of the bed, and leaned forward to gently wipe her tears with
the pad of my thumb. "Now, what's all this?"

She closed her eyes and groaned. Her cries intensified,

growing into full-fledged sobs. She struggled to speak through her tears. "It's too much! I can't...I can't. It's too soon." She collapsed against my chest as her entire upper body shook with her cries.

What in the holy holly was happening here? Whatever it was, it did not seem to bode well for my mission.

At a loss, I let her cry for a little bit. I patted her shoulders and rubbed her back and waited until she had calmed down enough to be able to speak.

When her shoulders stopped shaking, I pulled her back so that I could see her face and wiped her tears again.

"Whatever it is, little elf, we can fix it together."

She shook her head. "I can't go with you to the North Pole, Yule. I can't. I can't meet your parents."

"Well, they will be very disappointed. They were looking forward to it. And my father will have words for me about it, I'm sure. But, no matter. We certainly can't have you going if you are this upset about it. That won't be any fun."

"I don't want to disappoint them. I want them to like me." She sniffled, wiping her face with her sleeve. "That's the problem."

"I'm not following."

"Your dad is Santa, and your mom is Mrs. Claus. And,"—she lowered her voice to a whisper—"I'm on the naughty list. I can't meet Santa while I'm on the naughty list. It's too embarrassing."

"Well, first of all, I'm Santa, now. Not my dad. And we've met. We've done more than just meet." I winked.

She met my rebuttal with a death glare and sighed heavily. "You know what I mean."

"I do," I agreed. "So, it's time to get you off the naughty list, then."

Hope lit her eyes, and she looked up at me with a

mixture of excitement and heavy suspicion. "How do we do that?"

"Well, that depends on why you are on the naughty list."

I snapped my fingers and the large leather-bound book that held my lists appeared in my lap, open to the page that held her info.

She peered over my shoulder with interest, and I snapped the book shut. "Tut tut. These lists are top secret and confidential. Look away."

"Fine." She pouted, turning her body so her back was facing me.

I opened the book again and read. "Well this isn't so bad. It says far too much cursing, a bit of out-of-control partying, a couple of parking tickets, and a lack of charitable actions."

"Lack of charitable actions? What's that mean?"

"Exactly what it sounds like. For instance, you know that nice veteran who hangs out in the parking garage of your work? When was the last time you did something nice for him? Or even, I don't know, treated him like a human being?"

"Nice veteran?" She scoffed over her shoulder. "You mean that alcoholic, homeless bum who is always pandering for his next drink?"

I shook my head and slammed the book closed. "See now, this is exactly why you are on the naughty list. But don't worry, we can fix it."

She turned to face me then, looking weary. "How do we do that? And how long will it take? It's almost Christmas!"

"Won't take long. Let's work on it tonight and tomorrow, and then tomorrow night we can head up to the North Pole, and you can meet my parents with a clean slate and a clear conscience."

"Tomorrow night?" She raised her eyebrows. "It's that easy?"

"Well now, I didn't say it was going to be easy. But if it's that important to you, we can do it."

"It's that important to me." She straightened her back and steeled her shoulders. "What do we need to do?"

"Well first, there needs to be absolution for your naughty deeds. The cursing, and the partying, and the parking tickets. I'm sure you can guess what that means."

She groaned. "Let me guess. A spanking?"

I nodded. "A big one."

She sighed, stood and walked out of the room. Before I could even ask where she had gone, she returned with the wooden spoon. She placed it in my hand, and threw herself prostate over the edge of the bed.

"Okay. I'm ready."

Oh dear. She had no idea what she was in for. I stood and placed the spoon on the bed near her head, making sure it was in her line of vision.

"Not so fast, little elf. Little girls get the spoon. Big girls get Santa's belt."

She turned over so fast I half expected her to get whiplash. "What?"

I rested my hands on my thick leather belt. "You heard me. If getting off the naughty list is your goal, you're going to have to take the spanking you have coming. And it's a doozy. The future Mrs. Claus must be pure as the driven snow."

She winced and rolled back over, burying her face in her bedcovers. Her words were muffled, but I could make them out through employing my mind-reading skills.

"Okay, but I'm scared."

I sat on the bed and rubbed her back. "I know. It's scary, and I'm not going to lie. It's going to hurt. But then it will be over, and after we work on some good deeds tomorrow, you should be free and clear of the naughty list."

"Okay." I could hear her voice trembling. It squeezed my

heart, but I knew this must be done. And I was happy it had been her decision before I had had to bring it up. It still wasn't going to be easy, though.

I stood and rolled up my sleeves, preparing to begin. She shot off the bed. "Wait!"

"Yes, little elf?" This was it. She was going to decide it wasn't worth it and demand I leave. Christmas would be ruined forever, and it would be all my fault. I braced myself for the worst. I had to stop myself from reeling when she launched her body at mine, wrapping her arms around me and leaning her head against my chest.

"I needed a hug first," she mumbled into my shoulder. My heart melted, and I wrapped my arms around her slight frame, holding her close. We stayed locked in a tight embrace for several minutes. Finally, she exhaled deeply, pulled back, and looked me in the eye. "I might call you Daddy. Or Santa Daddy. It could just slip out." She seemed apprehensive about this fact and seemed to be warning me.

I chuckled. "I'd be disappointed if you didn't, little elf."

11
Crystal

This was crazy. I was certifiably insane, offering myself up for a spanking with a belt, in exchange for getting my name off some mythical naughty list. And sobbing over meeting his parents while my name was on the aforementioned list...really?

Yule and his stupid Christmas magic and his candy-cane-flavored dick had really done a number on me. He must have put me under some sort of crazy spell. That was the only fathomable explanation, I told myself.

It had to be that. Because the alternative? Well, the alternative was that I really believed in Santa and things like naughty lists, and Christmas magic, and that I was actually putting stock in his insistence that I was the next Mrs. Claus. And I *wanted* it to be true! That was the real crazy part.

I was still arguing silently with myself when I felt Yule pull me away from his chest, and guide me into position over the foot of the bed.

I heard him pull his thick black belt from the loops of his velvet slacks, and I cringed. Was this really worth it? That belt was thick and looked heavy. It was wide enough to cover the length of my ass with one swat. Was I really voluntarily subjecting myself to this? Over a stupid list?

"It's not a stupid list," Yule countered, reading my mind again. "And this was your idea. You were the one nearly in hysterics over that 'stupid list' when I got here. You were the one who insisted you needed to get off the naughty list before you met my parents. That was all you, little elf."

"I didn't know what I was getting myself into," I squawked, as his hand fell hard against my ass. It had been less than a week since I had been spanked, and I already had forgotten how much it hurt.

He spanked me with his hand half a dozen times before I caught my breath and looked at him over my shoulder. "You said you were going to use your belt!"

"This is called a warm-up, little elf. Trust me. You'll thank me later."

"Hmph." Nerves took root in my belly, and I squirmed against the bed, missing the softness and intimacy of his lap.

"This sucks," I whined. "Can't I go over your knee like every other time?"

"Can't swing a belt very well from that position," Santa responded, pausing to rub my back. "I'm here, little elf. But just in case, here." He reached to my pillows, and handed me the stuffed Santa bear we had gotten at the mall. "Squeeze your teddy if you get scared."

The bear made me smile, and I buried my face in its fur as Santa pushed my leggings and panties down to my knees. I groaned and shivered. The room was cold, and I swore the chill made it hurt worse when he spanked the underside of my thighs with his large hand. It hurt even worse when he began to lecture. Or maybe it was my heart that hurt. Either way, it sucked. His words were sweet, but scary, and the pain had yet to break through my mental barriers to get me to that point where I could believe what he was saying, even though I wanted to. Lord, how I wanted to.

"Little elf. Soon you will be my Mrs. Claus. I know it deep in my soul. I spent thirty-nine years guarding my heart, and then you came along, and I fell head over heels for you within minutes. I never want you to lose your sass, your humor, or your heart. I love your little side, and your big side, and I hope to see them both as we navigate this crazy journey together for years to come. But, my dear, all that being said, as Mrs. Claus, you must hold yourself to a higher standard. And if you fall from that, I will be there to catch you, by way of my hand, my belt, or my spoon. Mrs. Claus can never be on the naughty list, and it is Santa's job to make sure that that never happens. This will be the first time you feel the lick of my belt upon your bare bottom, but it will not be the last. Do I make myself clear?"

"Yes, Santa! Crystal clear!" I hollered above the rhythmic smacking echoing through the room.

I found his promise to be scary but oddly reassuring. Still, between the pain in my ass, the butterflies in my stomach, and the conflict taking root in my heart, I was a wreck. Tears already welled in my eyes, and I knew that any more sweet words from him would send me over the edge.

He stopped now, rubbing first my lower back and then my aching backside. The intimacy of his touch was soothing, and I ached to call him Daddy. It was coming soon, I could feel it, and there was nothing I could do to stop it.

"It's okay to let go, little elf. It will be easier if you do," he told me even as he stood and grabbed his belt from the spot on the bed where he had discarded it. *Easy for him to say. He isn't the one about to get whaled on with a strap of leather as wide as his arm.*

"Holy Holly, you make it hard to be serious sometimes, you know that?" he chuckled, as he came to stand behind me once more. I could hear the leather as he doubled it over and snapped it once for good measure.

My stomach turned, my ass cheeks clenched, and my pussy tingled. I moaned in horror. The hazards of getting spanked, when you weren't mentally six, was that his no-

nonsense dominance and the way he was equally tender and harsh was actually quite sexy.

At least that's what I was thinking before the first clash of leather cracked against my ass. The pain was exquisite. The leather was forgiving and punishing all at once. I could feel the bite of the leather flatten the fleshiest part of my ass, and I could feel the relief as the belt retreated, and the skin bounced back into place. It was oddly horrid and sensual, and I had to hide a smile as I breathed through it. And then the second lash fell, in the exact same spot as the first, and all of my earlier thoughts were nulled by the explosion of pain.

"What in the hell? That fucking hurts!" I realized my mistake immediately, and I wasn't even surprised when my outcry was answered with two hard smacks of the belt across the crease of my thighs.

"Language, little elf," Santa scolded. "Do not forget why you are in this position in the first place."

"What in the H-E- double candy canes! That fruitcaking hurt!" I yelled.

I could almost hear him trying not to laugh.

"Not quite the response I am going for when I correct you," he scoffed, bringing the belt down again, five times in quick succession. The pain seemed to concentrate at the point of impact and then flower and spread, creating a warmth that covered my entire lower body.

"Okay, okay, okay! I get it! I'll be good!" I shrieked, even as the strap of leather whooshed through the air, right at its target.

"Not so fast, little elf. You have many years of bad behavior to make up for, don't you?"

The sternness in his tone and the pain in my ass awakened the little girl inside me, and his admonition brought a tear to my eye. "Yes, Santa Daddy," I whispered, hiding my face in my teddy's fur.

"Better. You need to remember you are not in control here. Santa Daddy is, and while I don't like to hurt you, getting your name off that list is my number one priority at the moment. I don't want anything getting in the way of us starting a beautiful future together, and the naughty list is the last obstacle. If you hadn't brought it up, I would have soon. You just sped up the timeline. Do you understand, my little elf?"

"Yes, Daddy." I left off the Santa this time, simply because it felt right, and braced myself for the onslaught of pain as he continued the spanking.

The belt was falling harder and faster now, making it hard to concentrate on his words. I took solace in the fact my ass felt like an inferno because that had to mean it would be over soon.

"Soon, little elf, you will be mine. All your past sins will be absolved through the sting of my leather belt, and you will have a fresh, shiny clean slate. And I know you're going to remember this lesson for a long time to come and do your very best to change your behavior in the future, aren't you?"

"Yes, Daddy!" I couldn't keep from crying now, and I spoke the words through yells of pain and sobs of shame.

I counted ten more as the belt continued its harsh lesson upon the stinging flesh of my ass, which somehow hadn't yet gone numb. I felt every lash. I almost cried with joy when I heard the clatter of the buckle as the strap of leather fell from his hands and hit the ground near my feet.

Santa Bear's rainbow fur was soaked from my tears. I pushed him away and grabbed at a pillow before Yule scooped me into his arms, sat on the edge of the bed, and settled me in his lap, letting my torched ass hang in the space between his legs, an action for which I was very grateful. The Santa suit was soft, but his thighs were hard and muscular, and did not make a comfortable sitting place for someone with a freshly spanked bottom.

"You did very well, little elf. I'm proud of you." Yule's beaming smile radiated the pride he spoke of and warmed my heart. That smile almost made the pain in my posterior worth it. Almost, but not quite.

I forced a rueful smile, and tucked a stray lock of wet hair behind my ear as I looked up at him tearfully. "What if that wasn't...you know, enough?" I whispered. The thought of taking any more of a spanking almost killed me, but when we were done, I wanted to be sure we were well and done. No round two needed.

Santa frowned, his eyebrows furrowing together, as he inhaled deeply. "You should see your bottom, little elf. But as for that spanking being enough, it won't be. Not on its own. That's why we need to get to bed very soon. We have a busy day of doing good deeds and spreading Christmas cheer ahead of us. But, first, let's get a snack, shall we? We skipped dinner."

"I'm not hungry," I protested, with a pout, sliding off his lap. It was true. I wasn't hungry at all. Not for food at least.

I placed myself on my knees between his, and rubbed his leg through the soft velvet, starting at his knees, and working up to his groin. When I moved to caress his package through the fabric of his slacks, he blocked me with his hand.

"Not tonight," he scolded, waving his finger back and forth in front of my face. "You were very naughty, and tonight was about punishment, and punishment only. It doesn't come with a side of pleasure. You'll do well to remember that."

Santa

December 20th, 2018

"I want a Tonka truck, Santa." The little towheaded boy on my lap was small for his five years and missing his two front teeth.

"Ho, ho, ho! Aaron, you've been such a good boy this year, Santa's gonna see what he can do, but there just might be a Tonka truck with your name on it come Christmas morning."

I could feel Crystal's eyes watching me from her spot in the serving line. Strands of hair had fallen loose from her ponytail, framing her face, her makeup had all but melted off, and sweat glistening on her forehead. She was positively beaming and had never looked more beautiful. Except when screaming my name mid orgasm, of course.

Aaron leaped off my lap, and I handed him a candy cane and sent him back to his mother.

The poor woman looked slightly panicked at my promise of a toy, and I wondered if she, too, was a nonbeliever. If she was, she would be my first stop after the New Year. Poor woman deserved a little hope in her life. And little Aaron? Well, he would be getting his Tonka truck. And a new coat as well.

"I thought you had mall Santas for this stuff." Crystals voice interrupted my musings, and I looked up to see her standing beside me, and that the line of kids had dwindled to nothing. Aaron had been the last one.

"I do, but we were here. My father always tried to put in a few appearances himself each year, especially at places like this. I will probably do the same. It was pretty fun, and very rewarding. Good works are good for the soul."

"Yeah, but you're Santa. You do good works all the time. Your entire life is based on good works."

"Very true, little elf. Very true. And that's why you were the one picking up litter, and delivering baskets, visiting nursing homes, and sweating your cinnamon buns off in that kitchen. Speaking of which, did you help with the cleanup?"

"Yes. But my feet hurt. Can we go home now?" Suddenly embarrassed, she lowered her voice to a whisper. "That is, I mean, if you think it is okay?"

I furrowed my brow and frowned in confusion. I was very tired. "If I think it is okay?"

"Yeah, you know, like if I'm off the naughty list? Could you check? I don't want to stop now if it turns out I only need to do one more thing."

I was dead on my feet, and naughty list or no, all I wanted to do was fall into bed beside her. "I'll check when we get back to your place, little elf. And if by some oddity your name is still on there, I know a little deed we can do before we leave for the North Pole tomorrow. In fact, we might do it anyway because it's the right thing to do."

"Okay." She frowned, looking torn. She wanted her name off that list, but I suspected she was more exhausted than I was.

I stood and took her hand, thanked the shelter directors, and walked out the front door. Once outside, I whisked her into an alley and teleported us home.

"Every muscle in my body aches, even ones I didn't know I had. And my blisters have blisters," I whined, stripping down to my bra and panties as Yule watched from his spot on my bed next to me.

"At least you're off the naughty list," Santa reminded me, grinning. True to his word, he had checked as soon as we arrived. It was good news, but at the moment, all I cared about was getting underneath a spray of hot water and climbing into bed.

"I need a shower," I announced, standing to stalk off to the bathroom.

Yule caught my arm and stopped me. "Where are you going, little elf?"

I looked at him as if he had grown two heads. He wasn't usually this slow. "I'm going to shower."

"I ran a bath for us. With Epsom salts. Good for achy muscles."

"What? When did you do that? And where did you get Epsom salts?"

Yule raised his eyebrows, and I shook my head at my own silliness. "Oh. Right. Santa. Well, come on, then."

He followed me into the bathroom. The tub was indeed filled with warm water, and the smells of spearmint and eucalyptus permeated the air.

"Scented Epsom salts?" I asked, turning to find him naked.

He shrugged and climbed into the tub, sliding down into the water. "Well, it's not peppermint, but it's good for you on a day like today."

"Mmmhhmm," I murmured, stripping off my bra and panties and stepping into the tub in front of him. I leaned back against his hard chest and moaned. The Epson salts were working, and I could already feel the achiness and tension fading.

"Oh, this was a good idea." I stretched out as much as I could, straightening my legs and resting them on the bathroom wall. I wiggled my toes.

"You deserved it, little elf. You did good today. I'm very proud of you."

His words warmed me from the inside out. I was proud of me, too.

"That was fun," I admitted. "It felt good, and everyone was so happy to see us, everywhere we went."

"Yes, they were, weren't they? Some of them don't get a lot of visitors, or they are in such a hard place they don't have a lot of self-confidence. They feel invisible. When someone gives them help of any sort, or even a smile or a kind word, it can make all the difference."

I sighed. "I need to be better." I knew Yule wasn't meaning to, but he was making me feel bad for all the years I had been less than kind to people around me, especially people like the ones we had met today.

"You will, little elf," Yule said confidently. "What was your favorite part of the day?"

"Well, duh. The shopping." I giggled. Besides picking up litter, visiting the elderly, and feeding the homeless, we had purchased hundreds of toys, dropping them off at angel trees and Toys for Tots bins all over town.

"I should have guessed. It's always the shopping."

"What was your favorite?" I asked, closing my eyes as I waited for his answer.

"My favorite?" I felt the rumble of his laughter against my back. "My favorite was meeting your friend Marcus."

Beyond doing good deeds for the less fortunate, Yule had insisted that I needed to experience the joy of picking out and giving the perfect gift. He had taken me to the mall, and told me to pick out anything I wanted for anyone I wanted. Because my family would have thought I was completely off my rocker, if I had showed up with a pile of presents, I chose Marcus. I had picked out a rainbow beanie and scarf, a cashmere sweater, and a special Harry Potter coffee mug I knew he would love. He was a secret Potter-head.

I had felt overly vulnerable showing up at his house with gifts, knowing that we had never exchanged them before, and that Marcus was about as anti-Christmas as I had been before Yule came along and turned my holiday spirit on his head.

And oh yeah, there was Yule himself. I showed up on Marcus's doorstop with a hunky Santa Claus.

Marcus hadn't even batted an eye when I did, though. He invited us in graciously, and even served cocoa almost as good as Santa's. His house was already decked out for the holiday, and he seemed to wince a little when he sat on the hard wooden barstool at his kitchen island, raising my earlier suspicions.

He had loved the gifts, and even surprised me with a porcelain teddy bear for my collection.

All those surprises had been more than enough, but my favorite one was when he pulled me away from Yule, and cornered me by the Christmas tree.

"Hot Santa looks pretty legit," he whispered, wiggling his eyebrows suggestively. "But he's not your usual type. Where did you meet him?"

"Oh you know, around the neighborhood," I answered, gesturing vaguely.

Marcus smirked. "Yeah, I don't think so, honey. Tell me this, did he make a believer out of you? You off the naughty list yet?"

I choked on my cocoa and turned to gape at him. Marcus often spoke in code and innuendo, but this seemed like too big a coincidence to just be another one of his silly speech patterns.

"Oh, close your mouth, child. You knew I was safe. That's why you brought him here."

"I mean, I guess, I thought maybe..." I chose my words carefully. "You seemed different lately, and he had mentioned something, I guess."

Marcus nodded sagely, bringing his mug to his lips and taking a sip before smiling. "Honey, I am always gonna be as gay as a Froot Loop, but I'll tell you one thing. Vixen the elf mistress can visit me anytime she wants to. In fact, here soon, I'm going to start actively trying to get back on that list for next year. Mmmhmm."

I laughed, and shook my head. "He broke into my apartment and started spanking me."

Marcus nodded, looking totally unsurprised.

"He says I'm his Mrs. Claus."

Marcus turned and peeked at Yule over his shoulder before turning back to me. "Girl! Go get your Santa then, you lucky bitch."

I smiled and craned my neck to look up at 'my Santa.' "Yeah, okay. That part was my favorite, too. So Vixen the elf mistress is real, huh?"

Santa grinned. "Well, little elf, it's like I said. Somebody has to help the naughty boys see the error of their ways. Sometimes a little Santa magic is enough, but if it isn't, a visit from Vixen will usually do the trick."

"You're crazy." I stretched my body to receive his offered kiss.

"Yeah," he agreed. "But it's the good kind of crazy."

12
Crystal

"Onward to the North Pole," Santa cried, as we climbed into his jet-powered sleigh.

I smiled weakly. I was excited, of course, but nervous as all get-out. I had been stalling all morning, first by insisting we make breakfast together then by taking as long as possible to choose the perfect outfit, and finally by reminding him of the errand he said we would run this morning. It had turned out to be delivering food, clothes, and money, along with a hotel-room key to the homeless veteran I passed on my way to work every day. His name, I learned, was Mac, and he was a pretty good guy who had had a run of bad luck. Lesson learned.

I had learned a lot of lessons over the past ten days, many of them the hard way, but I was proud of the changes I had made. I was different, now, and ready to face my future, however unbelievable it might be.

It was a good thing I was ready, too, because the sleigh ride was short and fast, and before I could finish my musings or take a deep breath or worry about whether or not I had picked the right outfit, we were there.

The sleigh landed atop a hill of snow in front of a large majestic-looking log-cabin-style home, with a huge wrap-around porch. Christmas lights framed every inch of the awning and all of the windows. In the distance was a matching building. It was slightly larger. A large sign hung in front of the door, proclaiming it to be *Santa's Workshop*.

I couldn't help but feel the magic of Christmas here. It lit up my soul, and warmed me from the inside out.

"Oh my goodness. It's a real winter wonderland. I've never seen anything like this before," I breathed. Being from the desert and not traveling much had really limited my exposure to snow and cold. I shivered and pulled my jacket tight. I'd never been so cold in my life, but the snow was calling to me, and I wanted to play. As soon as the sleigh stopped completely, I stood to climb out.

Santa caught me by my elbow before I could get anywhere. "Where are you going?"

"I want to play in the snow." I tugged slightly, trying to free myself from his grasp.

"Not dressed like that, little elf. You'll turn into a popsicle." Snapping his fingers, he completely changed my adorable "meet the parents" outfit into a full-on snowsuit, complete with bulky boots, gloves, a scarf, and a hat that covered my ears. All bright red, of course.

"Are you for real? I feel like that kid in that movie we watched the other night where his mom wraps him up. I can barely move." I dramatically waddled like a penguin in place.

"You'll thank me later. Trust me."

I was already ten times warmer than I had been and wondering why he hadn't bundled me up sooner, but I wasn't going to tell him that. Judging by the smug look on his face, he already knew, anyway.

I looked at him, gave a huge smile, and thought, *Bite me, Santa Daddy,* before turning my attention back to the snow.

"Careful, little elf, or I might do that," he growled from behind me.

There was about a foot of snow on either side of the walkway, and I trudged right into it. It felt like trying to walk through a pool, but without that floating feeling. I stood there for a minute, taking it all in. Then I closed my eyes and free-fell backward. The snow crunched under my weight, and I sank down into it. It was soft and cold, and I loved it.

Giggling, I spread my arms and legs out wide in a sweeping motion to make a snow angel. The suit Santa had wrapped me in was serious business. It kept all the cold and wet out.

"Have you ever built a real snowman?" I asked from my sprawled position. Getting up wasn't as easy as getting down had been, and I struggled as I tried to stand.

Ignoring my predicament, Santa guffawed. "I grew up here, little elf. I'm a snowman-building Jedi master."

"Show me!"

"Not right now, little elf. We don't really have time. We're going to be discovered any second now. If they aren't already watching through the window. Come on." He grabbed my hand and pulled me out of the snow, effortlessly.

Meeting his parents was the reason we were here, of course, but we had all day, and I wasn't ready. The North Pole and the splendor of the snow had brought out that buried little girl, and I wanted to play.

"Come on!" I tugged on his arm, pulling it up and down. "Just show me really quick. We'll build a little baby snowman. It doesn't have to be fancy or anything. How long can it possibly take?"

"Long enough, little elf. Let's go."

Shaking off my arm, he turned and walked toward the house, but I wasn't ready. Panic seized me with every step he took.

I followed slowly, ten steps behind. The snow crunched under my boots, and I was inspired. Stopping to eyeball a big mound at the base of a bush near the porch, I allowed my impulses to take over. Bending down, I took a big scoop of it into my hands, and quickly formed it into a ball.

"Hey, Daddy," I yelled, chucking the ball of snow in his

direction when he turned toward me to see what was the matter.

The ball of snow made a satisfying thudding sound when it hit the shoulder of his velvet Santa coat.

He cocked an eyebrow at me and smiled. "Oh, little elf, you have made a grave mistake."

I didn't wait for him to say anything else before I reloaded, aimed, and let another one fly. This time, I hit him square in the chest. Before I could finish packing the third one, Santa charged and tackled, sending me flying backward, ass first into the snow. He leaned over me, knocking me all the way back, and pinned my arms above my head on either side.

"Now, now, now. What do we have here?" The voice was a deep rumble, and my stomach sank as I guessed the origin. "Could it be my son, and my future daughter-in-law having a bit of fun without me? A snowball fight, perhaps?" I looked up to see a handsome white-haired man of nearly eighty, with a big belly and a full beard, wearing jeans and a thick red-and-green plaid flannel. The scarf wrapped around his neck matched the jacket of Yule's suit, and I groaned. This was not the first impression I wanted to make.

"Get off her, Son," he boomed. "The elves could be watching." It seemed a weird thing to say, and I giggled as Yule rolled off me, and helped me up.

As soon as I was standing, his father advanced toward me, grabbing my hands in his. I was shocked to see that there were tears in his eyes, and his features were fraught with emotion.

"Crystal." His voice cracked. "I've been waiting for this day for a long time. I'm so sorry about your father, and I'm so sorry I wasn't able to grant your Christmas wishes all those years ago."

My mouth dropped open as a tear tracked down his face.

I felt myself start to tear up in response to his genuine emotion. "Oh, no," I whispered. "I was just a little girl. I didn't understand. It's okay. Please don't cry."

He cried harder, pulling me into his arms for a tight bear hug. It felt lovely. He was soft and warm and smelled like Yule, but older and more mature. There was a faint hint of sandalwood mixed in with all the Christmas.

His tears were warm and wet against my cheek, and my heart broke for this sweet man who had the weight and wishes of all the world's children on his shoulders.

"I've waited so long for this day," he repeated in my ear. He finally pulled back, clasping both of my hands between his and beamed at me. "Well, little elf, you finally got your Daddy now, haven't you? I'm sorry you had to wait so long, but I know my boy will spend every day proving he was worth the wait."

My eyes narrowed in confusion as I weighed the meaning behind his words. I glanced at Yule in question. Had he told his father everything? Yule shook his head. His eyebrows were raised high, and his mouth was set in a flat line. I looked back at his father, and he winked at me.

"You knew?"

Santa, the elder Santa, threw back his head and laughed, a merry ho ho ho. "Of course I knew. I'm Santa." He said this as if it was of no consequence. "As soon as I read those letters, I knew. I couldn't grant your wishes back then. I couldn't give you the daddy you needed. Not for a long time, anyway. But you got him, didn't you?"

He looked back and forth between the two of us with a smirk.

For a brief moment, irritation rushed through me, and I read the same emotion on Yule's face as we realized we had been set up in a conspiracy that dated back two full decades, if not longer. Our eyes met, and then we laughed. Deep, rolling belly laughs. The elder Santa joined in, and soon Mrs. Claus appeared, beaming, in her red dress, with rosy-red cheeks.

She didn't say a word, or bother to introduce herself. She simply took me in her arms and pulled me close against her generous chest, patting my hair, and murmuring about how happy she was to meet me. She called me her successor, and I waited for the clutch of panic and anger I always felt when Yule made reference to my being Mrs. Claus. It didn't come.

"See?" Yule teased, taking my hand, and pulling me away from his mother. "It's destiny. It's been destiny from the very beginning. Before dating or marrying was a thought in either of our heads. You were always mine. You just didn't know it yet."

"Yeah, yeah, yeah. So, I'm yours. It's destiny. Fate. Written in the stars, etcetera and so forth. The point has been made." I was teasing, too, but serious. I wiggled my eyebrows at him and giggled. "So, what are you going to do about it?"

"This." Yule, in his Santa suit, dropped to one knee in front of me. He snapped his fingers, and a ring box appeared in his hand.

I gasped aloud. I'd known it was going to happen. It was simple deduction, of course, but now that it was really happening, I couldn't breathe.

This is crazy, I told myself, beginning to head down that spiral of reality. I had met this man only ten days prior. There were a million reasons this would not work. But God, I wanted it to.

"Crystal Angelina Turner." Yule took my hand in his, and kissed the top of it before continuing. "We may not have known each other long, but we have the rest of our lives to get to know each other better. We are, as you say, written in the stars. You are my fate, my destiny, and my soul mate. Will you also be my Mrs. Claus? Marry me."

When he spoke, he looked into my eyes, and I could see the love shining out from his soul as he gazed up at me. I got lost in those blue eyes of his, and all my doubts and worries melted away.

"This is crazy," I answered, shaking my head. "But the good kind of crazy." I mirrored his earlier words back to him. "Yes, Santa Daddy, I will marry you. I can't wait to be your Mrs. Claus."

Yule jumped to his feet, a smile on his face as he gave a cry of victory before gathering me in his arms, lifting me off my feet, and spinning me around in a circle. Then he set me down and kissed me so deeply, I don't think I imagined that my boots sank down into the snow.

When we finally broke apart, his father cleared his throat and I blushed. I had forgotten we had an audience.

The elder Santa stood there, Mrs. Claus by his side, wiping his eyes with the edge of his red velvet scarf. "Now that," he choked out between tears, "is what I call a happy ending. A real Christmas miracle."

Epilogue
Crystal

December 25th, 2018

"He sees you when you're sleeping."

I was awakened to Santa's gruff voice singing in my ear. Moaning, I turned to cuddle into his warmth, pressing my body against his. I frowned when I realized he was still wearing his Santa suit. I tugged at it, pulling the jacket open to lay my head against his bare chest. He chuckled and kissed the top of my head.

"Or when you're not sleeping, as was the case with you last night, naughty girl. You were supposed to rest."

I opened my eyes as much as I could, as they were still heavy with sleep. I wasn't sure when I had finally gone to bed, or how much sleep I had gotten, but it had been pretty late, and I suspected it wasn't much.

I had spent most of the night packing, in between stalking my brand-new husband using a Santa tracker app on my phone. I knew it wasn't accurate, but it helped me count down the hours until he would be home and officially on vacation. The hours until we could start our honeymoon and our new life together. This man was my husband now. The wedding had been small and lovely, a quiet and intimate ceremony the morning before, at the North Pole, before the Christmas craziness officially commenced.

Once I had stopped fighting what he insisted was my destiny, my entire outlook on life had changed. I'm not sure when it happened, exactly, as the entire romance between us had been a crazy whirlwind of emotion, but the love I had for him consumed me, and I felt like it was easier to breathe when he was around. He made me a better person.

"Now I can rest with you," I countered, snuggling in even closer than before. "You need to rest, too, after your long night."

Yule shook his head and hooked my chin with the crook of his finger.

"I will, later. Right now, I want to watch you open presents."

At the mention of gifts, I sprang up in bed. It was my first ever real Christmas morning, and he had promised it would be amazing.

"Are there presents?"

"Mountains of them." He grinned widely when he answered.

"Eeep!" I squealed and jumped off the bed, sprinting to the door, and down the short hallway to the living room. "Holy holly!" The small pile of packages under the tree had more than tripled in size overnight. "What are you doing? Making up for lost time? Geez!" Staring at the pile of gifts, I almost felt silly for being so excited. I truly was acting like a child on Christmas morning, but I could not help myself.

"When Daddy makes a promise, he keeps it, little elf," he whispered into my ear.

I turned and threw my arms around his neck. "Can I open them all? Right now?"

He tightened his arms around me and lifted me off my feet. "Nope, not until you earn them." He wiggled his eyebrows.

I eyed him dubiously. "How?"

"Oh, I think you know. Christmas morning candy sticks should be our first new tradition as husband and wife," he quipped.

"Presents first," I huffed. "If you wanted to do that first, we could have just stayed in bed. But you lured me out here to this pile of presents, and now I want to open them. If they are really good, maybe you'll earn some bonus points for later."

Yule guffawed loudly, kissed my cheek, and leaned in to whisper in my ear. "If I get enough bonus points, do I get to shove my candy stick in your Hershey hole?"

I was still sputtering when he set me down on my feet, turned me toward the tree, and got me moving with a loud slap across my bottom.

"Ow!" I exclaimed, turning to glare at him. "We don't have time for all of that, anyway. After presents, I need to finish packing so we can move to the North Pole in time for the New Year's celebration. I promised your mother."

Santa took a step back and looked around the room at my piles of half-packed boxes. "Silly girl, did you forget your Daddy has magical powers?"

With a smile and a wink, he lifted his hand between us and snapped his fingers. In a second, the entire room was empty save for the Christmas tree and the surrounding presents.

I shook my head, and rolled my eyes, wagging a finger as I teased him. "Silly Santa, I thought real daddies did things the hard way."

He gaped at me, feigning wounded shock. "I worked all night! I traveled all over the world and back again and delivered millions of presents. I'm tired. Plus, there's only one thing Santa Claus wants to do the hard way on Christmas morning, little elf, and that's Mrs. Claus."

Did you enjoy Santa Daddy?

Don't miss the first two books in the Fantastical Daddy Dom series?

Check out Genie Daddy!

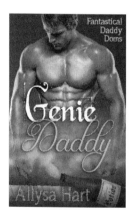

Genie Daddy, Fantastical Daddy Doms Book 1

I lost everything, was shipped off to live with an aunt I barely knew, and was put to work cleaning her dilapidated antique shop.

And then, I met Callum.

Or should I say I released him?

I was a socialite with a strong sense of entitlement and a lot of anger.

He was a Dominant genie with a hard body and an even harder hand.

It could never work.

Could it?

Check out Ogre Daddy!

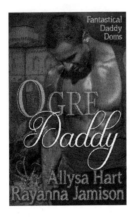

Ogre Daddy: Fantastical Daddy Doms Book 2

The princess was destined to be mine. She just didn't know it yet.

Sparks fly, skirts go up and panties come down. My stubborn princess will learn that her Ogre Daddy is determined to turn our nightmare into the ultimate happily ever after.

Rayanna Jamison

Writing has been a passion of mine since I was 9 years old, and I always dreamed of becoming an author, but life happens and sometimes that first step seems like a giant leap. I credit a life changing move from the Oregon to Utah in the fall of 2013 as the catalyst that began my writing career.

I now reside in Southern Utah with my husband, my two children, two dogs, my mother, my 92 year old grandfather and a lizard named Leo.

I write what I love to read, which is fun romantic stories about submission in its many forms, and often joke that my stories get slightly dirtier with each one I write. When I am not writing, I enjoy my passions, which include cooking, drinking good coffee and good wine, shopping for crazy knee socks, celebrating with sushi for every occasion, and most of all spending time with my friends and family.

Stalk Me Links

Facebook: goo.gl/8LJxBB
Amazon: goo.gl/m4Y7X2
Bookbub: goo.gl/KwFPCA
Instagram: goo.gl/5BXfX9
Twitter: goo.gl/WpkuVX
Reader Group: goo.gl/H7e5LN
Newsletter: goo.gl/ACZNPi

Also By
Rayanna Jamison

Love Multiplied Series

Green Valley Brides

Luke's First Bride

Luke's Rogue Bride

Corbins Bend

A Perfect Partnership- Corbin's Bend Season 2

Ginger Up- Corbins's Bend Season 3

A Holiday Ruse- Corbin's Bend Season 4

Vegas Nights Series

Collared

Claimed

Second Chance Ranch Series

Winterland Daddies

Spring Fever Daddies

Other Books by Rayanna Jamison

Catching Her Cowboy Daddy

Cole for Christmas

Santa Sir

Collections

Sweet Town Love (with various authors)

12 Naughty Days of Christmas (with various authors)

12 Naughty Days: A Holiday Collection (with various authors)

A Spanking Good New Year (with various authors)

Masters of The Castle: Witness Protection Program (with various authors)

Other Uses for a Wooden Spoon: A Corbin's Bend Cookbook

Allysa Hart

I am a full-time mom to two sassy, strong-willed, loveable little girls. What can I say? They take after their mama. I'm on the wrong side of thirty, I have been married to my best friend for over ten years and I can't imagine doing life with anyone else by my side. We are Southern California transplants, currently residing in a very rural part of the East Coast. I have two crazy dogs that I adore, even though they drive me out of my ever-loving mind most days.

Writing and graphic design consume all of my spare time, and I could not be happier. This journey I am on is a crazy one, but I wouldn't trade it for the world.

Make sure you don't miss out on any of my newest releases by signing up for my newsletter! You can also stalk me all over social media.

Facebook
Instagram
Twitter
Tumblr
Pinterest
BookBub

Also by
Allysa Hart

A Rose in Bloom

Adopting Katie

Katie's New Daddy

Genie Daddy

Ogre Daddy

Masters of the Castle: Witness Protection Program

Paris Heat

Printed in Great Britain
by Amazon